SQUASH
The Ambitious Player's Guide

$9.91

SQUASH
The Ambitious Player's Guide

ALAN COLBURN

faber and faber
LONDON · BOSTON

First published in 1981
by Faber and Faber Limited
3 Queen Square London WC1N 3AU
Second edition revised in 1984

Printed in Great Britain by
Fletcher & Son, Norwich

British Library Cataloguing in Publication Data

Colburn, Alan
  Squash.—2nd ed.
  1. Squash rackets (Game)
  I. Title
  796.34'3   GV1004

  ISBN 0-571-13361-4

To my friends who helped me

Contents

Acknowledgements

The author wishes to thank the following newspapers for permission to print copyright material: *The Times*; *The Sunday Times*; the *Observer* and *Squash Player International*. Thanks are also due to Random House Inc. for permission to print excerpts from *On Sport* by J. A. Michener (1976); Simon and Schuster Ltd for permission to print excerpts from *Running and Being: The Total Experience* by G. A. Sheehan, MD; Hutchinson Publishing Group Ltd (Stanley Paul) for excerpts from *The Complete Middle Distance Runner* by D. Watts, H. Wilson and F. Horwill (1974); Minerva Bookshop for excerpts from *Run to the Top* by A. Lydiard and G. Gilmour.

The author and publishers would also like to thank Messrs G. de Braak and M. Niland for supplying the photographs used in this book.

Preface to Second Edition

The first edition was written when Geoff Hunt was undisputedly the world's number one squash player. Since then Jahangir has burst onto the scene and at present there seem to be no other real contenders for his crown. His advisers must have noted why Zaman failed to beat Geoff consistently and trained Jahangir such that he would not fail, given his talents, in his quest for total domination of the squash world. Just prior to the epic final between Hunt and Jahangir in the British Open of 1981, the latter was reported to have said that he was looking forward to a three-hour encounter. In other words, Geoff's marvellous physical abilities held no fear for the much younger contender. Geoff did win in four games which lasted two hours and twelve minutes, but only after coming back from what looked like the brink of total exhaustion.

Zaman is still one of the top players in the world and he has enthralled many galleries with the severity of his play. Perhaps he was all too aware of the toll that training programmes and matches similar to those of Hunt, Barrington, Brownlee and Brumby could exact, to have been an undisputed world number one.

Despite having had the pleasure of watching Jahangir closely, there has not been a great deal that I wished to change in this edition. What I have done is to re-write certain sections where I felt I could express myself better and add passages, most significantly in the last chapter which has been appreciably extended.

Introduction

This book is designed to help the ambitious squash player achieve his or her goal. It is not intended primarily for the absolute beginner although the basics of the game are dealt with in Part I. The total beginner would be advised first to work through an introductory book to squash.

Chapter 1 looks at the grip, working from first principles to considering unorthodox grips, ways of exploiting a biased grip, and the pros and cons of changing the grip during a rally.

The two following chapters are devoted to the forehand and backhand drives. It is recommended that advanced players, players of good club-level standard, gloss over these and move on to the chapters which deal with the other shots. Emphasis is placed upon explaining why certain aspects of stroke production are important, rather than upon laying down the law as regards the correct technique. In the final analysis it is the result of the shot that counts—I have seen too many great players, who have employed vastly differing techniques, to have written this section in a dogmatic fashion. The fact that there are various ways of hitting the ball should stimulate the reader to experiment himself and, in this way, he might discover a technique for striking the ball that better suits him. It is hoped that merely describing the different shots can expand the acquisitive reader's range of strokes and, possibly, improve his ability to deceive. Throughout the book, I have attempted to present as *wide* an array of ideas as possible to encourage the reader to *think* and to choose those appropriate to his game.

Although some chapters in Part II are devoted solely to discussions of movement, shot patterns and deception, brief references will be made to these factors in earlier chapters covering the various strokes. The established player might well prefer to start reading the book from Chapter 9, which deals with the vital, yet rarely considered, area of movement. He could then peruse the earlier chapters by way of a refresher course.

Chapters 10 and 11 encompass a discussion on shot patterns and deception. With this knowledge, you are better able to experiment with new shots and techniques, in fact to be a more positive player, because you realize, for example, the conditions under which you can attack the front of the court.

Chapters 12 to 15 deal with training. They include a warm-up routine and the rationale behind it, and training without and with the ball (both on and off court). Practice routines with the ball, both solo and dual, are described in detail. Guidelines have been given to enable the reader to devise the mix and volume of training best suited to his ambitions and present physical condition. The language used is simple enough for the layman, and references have been given so that the interested reader may pursue certain topics in greater depth.

Complementing the discussion, the potential for weight training is explored and schedules are described which should lead to a more balanced and improved development of the body. As an example of a top player's training programme, Geoff Hunt's preparation for the 1978 British circuit—which culminated in his winning the British Open—is described.

Possibly the most neglected area in training, namely that of improving or ensuring flexibility, is dealt with in Chapter 15. A flexible body is vital to minimize injuries particularly as one grows older or as one trains harder.

Finally, 'Just Talking' is literally that. From my travelling as a touring professional, from coaching and from being associated with the game and many fine players over the years, I have accumulated many useful pieces of information or advice.

Although I have used as my 'player' a right-handed male, what has been written also applies, obviously with simple adjustments, to left-handers and to the ladies. The book was written with the thought, 'how do the best players in the world train and play', very much in my mind. In this vein, I have tried to highlight points made, as often as possible, with drawings of action photographs. These illustrations reinforce the view that there is no one *best* way of hitting the ball—after all, we are not all built the same. They will also help the reader to form a mental picture of what he is trying to do. I have found this mental image an enormous aid when trying to improve my own technique.

After each chapter a brief summary of the salient points of the chapter is given.

Part I

1. The Grip

WHEN INTRODUCED, SHAKE HANDS FIRMLY

The racket should be firmly gripped as if you were shaking hands with it—the 'V', between the index finger and the thumb, should be approximately in the centre of the grip. The base of the 'V' should be on the left bevel of the grip, and the fingers spread (see Fig. 1).

The base of the grip should fit snugly into the base of the fleshy pad to the left of the 'life-line'. To grip the racket half-way up the handle does not seem to be worth the improved racket-head control as the player has to move that much further to the ball on each occasion. Moreover, because the hand is that much closer to the head the player can generate less power than when using a conventional grip.

THE RIDGE IN THE BASE OF THE GRIP

There seem to be no hard and fast advantages or disadvantages in building up the base of the racket. There are as many players who play with a raised base as without one. Personally, I prefer a raised base as the racket feels more secure in my hand—that is, it is less likely to slip out. Other players may well prefer a smooth tail-end as it might facilitate

Left bevel or edge of the grip

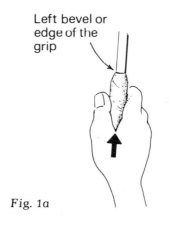

Fig. 1a

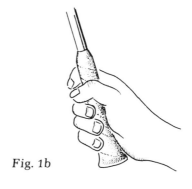

Fig. 1b

Fig. 1c

13

gripping the racket more tenuously than usual to ensure reaching that 'certain winner'. I am convinced, however, that these advantages are all in the mind and that one prefers whatever one is used to. In any event, players should experiment with and without these ridges—it is a simple task to remove or build in the ridge.

LEATHER, REVERSE LEATHER, TOWELLING OR SUEDE?

Most top players prefer towelling grips which, when damp, provide a better surface to grip than does, for example, leather. There is a new suede grip called 'Aquagrip', which has been introduced on to the market. It has the advantage of lasting longer than the towelling grip and it has a less smooth surface than plain leather. I have not played often enough with it to assess how it performs when the hands really start to perspire, however it is certainly worth trying. Most professionals carry a little brush (a nail brush will do) which they use to roughen the surface of the towelling grip before and during games. Players using leather grips may well roughen the grip with a key or on any suitably rough surface, for example, a brick.

Players bothered with sweating hands should use towelling sweat-bands (wristlets) or one of the many available types of resin powder to ensure a steady grip. I have found the use of a wristlet on either hand useful in hot and humid conditions. The left wristlet can be used to wipe the brow, thus avoiding the saturation of the

right wristlet. It may well be helpful to change wristlets in between games. It is certainly advantageous to have a couple of rackets with which you are equally at home, so that you can change rackets in between games.

GRIP SIZE AND SHAPE

The cardinal principle in choosing a racket with the correct grip size and shape is that it must feel good. Currently it is the fashion amongst top players to play with grips about 10 cm (4 in) in circumference. This, in most cases, allows the index finger to fit snugly alongside the side of the thumb without the finger-nail cutting into the thumb. It also allows the other fingers to reach comfortably close to the base of the thumb (see Fig. 1b).

As regards the shape of the grip, most players would be advised to become accustomed to the shape of the racket with which they play. Changing the shape of a grip does alter the balance of the racket and if you have more than one racket it is not easy to alter both grips in exactly the same fashion. In summary then, leave tinkering with the shape of the grip to the experts.

EXPLOITING AN EXAGGERATED GRIP

You will recall that I advocated a grip with the 'V' 'approximately' centred. Why should one centre the 'V'? Consider a grip with the 'V' far to the right: that is, if you grip the racket with the head vertical to the floor and the shaft parallel to it, so that you see only a little of the knuckle of the index finger. If you try to hit the ball with this grip you will notice that it is most comfortable to strike the forehand relatively early in relation to the body. Conversely, it is most comfortable to strike the backhand relatively late in relation to the body. The impact is late relative to the centred grip. Figures 2–4 should illustrate this. Note that the position of the line

Fig. 4

Fig. 2
Fig. 3

on the court illustrates the comfortable impact area.

Now hold the racket so that you see four knuckles. You will find that it is most natural to strike the forehand a little later in relation to your body. Conversely, you are comfortable striking the backhand a little earlier in relation to your body (see Figs. 5–7).

Fig. 5

15

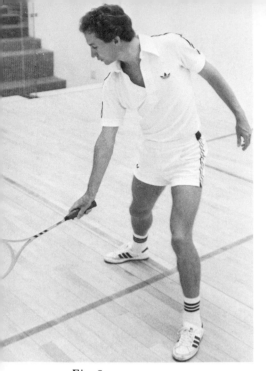

Fig. 6

Bearing this in mind, one should always note an opponent's grip. Very often in the lower leagues, players have very biased grips. This implies that they are strong in two corners of the court and relatively weak in the other two. For example, a player with a grip with the 'V' far to the left (showing four knuckles) is stronger in the left-front corner and in the right-back corner. Conversely, he is weaker in the right-front corner and in the back-left corner. An astute player would tend to concentrate his attack and, in fact, defence in these areas, striving to work his opponent on the diagonal shown in Fig. 8.

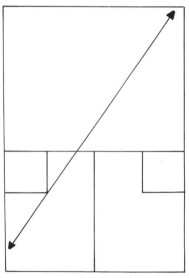

Fig. 8

CHANGING YOUR GRIP

Could not the above information be used to strengthen a player in all areas of the court? To the average club player the answer has to be 'No'. He will not have the time

Fig. 7

to change his grip during a rally nor will he be able to spend enough time on court to familiarize himself with this sophisticated gambit. Thus the advice to a club player must be to maintain a centred grip which has no obvious potential weaknesses.

Gogi Alauddin and Jonah Barrington must be the best-known exponents of changing their grips. They will shorten their grip, that is grip the racket nearer the head, and rotate it to help extricate a good length ball from the back of the court. In Fig. 9 Jonah Barrington is shown getting himself out of trouble. A shortened grip allows him to manipulate the racket head more effectively in a confined area, and the rotated grip makes it easier to play the ball late in relation to his body. In this fashion, Jonah is often able to surprise his opponent, who expects a weak boast (a shot which hits the side wall first) from the back of the court, by producing a lob down the side wall. Thus Jonah often manages to turn a defensive position into an attacking one.

SUMMARY

* Grip the racket as if shaking hands—spread the fingers.
* Ensure that the handle does not slip in your hand during a match. If it does, experiment with a new grip material, sweat-bands, alternating rackets between games, and the 'sure grip' powders.
* Grip size should be such that it allows the forefinger to nestle comfortably alongside the thumb.
* Exploit any marked bias in your opponent's grip.
* For the average player, there is not time to change the grip during a rally.

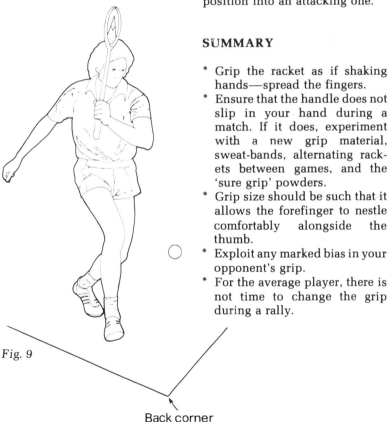

Fig. 9

Back corner

2. The Forehand Drive

CLASSIC IMAGE

A coach should always strive to show very simply the basic principles involved in hitting the forehand drive. An established player may be helped by being told that he has 'ineffective forearm pronation' (the coach will preferably explain himself more simply). However, telling the average player what to do in the hitting area will merely produce a disjointed and awkward swing. Thus coaches have long used the image of throwing a ball in explaining the technique required in hitting a forehand.

BALL-THROWING TECHNIQUE

Let us examine in some detail why the ball-throwing image is so useful. Firstly, one usually throws with the feet well spread to provide a firm and balanced base for the arm action. Secondly, the shoulders are turned so that the weight and muscles of the body are brought into action, complementing the muscles of the arm and wrist. Thirdly, the wrist is brought into action just before the ball leaves the hand. Fourthly, the ball leaves the hand approximately level with the front knee. And finally there is the follow-through—the hand flying on towards the target.

For some readers it will be unnecessary to translate the relevance of these points to the squash action but, as basic principles can never be stressed enough, the reasons for this technique are given below.

BACKSWING

A forehand drive starts with the backswing. A backswing is needed primarily because time is required to generate racket-head speed to power the ball. Furthermore, a backswing stretches the muscles that are to be employed in generating racket-head speed. A stretched muscle or ligament fibre is capable of a greater workload.

The shoulders are turned to bring muscle groups, other than the arm, into action to power the ball. Perhaps the most important reason for turning the shoulders is that it will encourage a racket arc which passes close to the body. This will assist the player in extricating the ball which has been struck to a good length—suggestions regarding this aspect of squash are covered in Chapter 9: Movement. The turning of the shoulders also assists in transferring the weight from the right leg to the left leg. A correct 'top of the backswing' position—illustrating the shoulder turn, transference of weight and wrist position—can be seen in Fig. 10.

Fig. 10

Observant squash enthusiasts may recognize that some of the current top players, for example Hiddy Jahan, do not have cocked wrists at the top of their backswings. But a careful study of their swings will show that at the start of the downswing they cock their wrists. One thing that Hiddy does is to wind up well so that he can hit the ball with force.

STARTING THE DOWNSWING

Returning to the idea of throwing a ball, you will notice that you

Fig. 12. Incorrect

begin the throwing movement with the base of the palm leading. You can see how this is translated to the squash stroke in Fig. 11. Players who have recently converted from tennis may find it useful to consider beginning the downswing leading with the elbow (see Fig. 13). Remember to cock your wrist and avoid the starting and hitting positions shown in Figs. 12 and 14.

Fig. 11

Fig. 13

19

Fig. 14. Incorrect

Figs. 15a, b, c

HITTING AREA

We now come to the vital hitting area where, to use Geoff Hunt's terminology, the fore-arm is pronated, and also where the wrist is brought into action to whip the ball away. The meaning of the fore-arm pronation is best explained using illustrations (see Fig. 15). It is worth noting the elbow position and wrist cock in this sequence. Rather than think and puzzle about this, however, if you remember the ball-throwing technique, that is exactly what you would do!

If you are trying to generate pace, always try to have your body weight moving in the direction you wish the ball to take. To achieve maximum power, you should strike the ball whilst the racket head is accelerating, hence you wish to strike the ball somewhere near the plane which

would travel through the inside of your left knee (see Fig. 16). Again, to achieve maximum power, the player must hit right 'through' the ball (see Fig. 17). A full follow-through, ending with the racket head high in the air, is an excellent indicator of a correct swing, and is also necessary to avoid endangering one's opponent. The danger arises when the follow-through is flat (see Fig. 18), often the result of generating power with the arm alone. As the player will tend to fall away from the ball, the timing of the stroke is likely also to be poor. The most obvious danger is, however, that to the opponent.

Fig. 16

Fig. 18. Incorrect

SUMMARY

* A useful image is that of throwing a ball or skimming a pebble across a lake.
* A high backswing, with turned shoulders, stretches the relevant muscle groups and enlarges the racket arc.
* Do not drop the wrist at the start of the downswing.
* To achieve power, the transfer of weight should be in the direction in which the ball is struck.
* Hit right through the ball and finish high.

Fig. 17

3. The Backhand Drive

No easy metaphor springs to mind when teaching the backhand. There is no hit it 'as if you were....' Yet most of the top players in the world have superior ball control on their backhands. Possibly this is because so many players attack the backhand without really thinking and thus the backhand is played so much more than the forehand. More probable, however, is the fact that the right shoulder moves less than during a forehand drive.

THE SIMPLE WAY

One simple and effective way of teaching the backhand (see below) was shown to me by Mike Corby, a great British sportsman and coach. Start out with your feet about 45 cm (18 in) apart along the line that divides the back of the court into two. Grip the racket and rest it on the left shoulder (see Fig. 19a). Note the racket-head position and the way the wrist is 'cocked'. Keeping the racket and arm in this position, and without moving your left foot, step forward and sideways with the right leg (see Figs. 19b and c).

The same principles given in the previous chapter apply. Briefly, the shoulders are turned to ensure that the racket head travels through a big arc, to bring muscles, other than the arm, into action, and to facilitate the weight

Fig. 19a. Note the racket-head position and the way the wrist is cocked

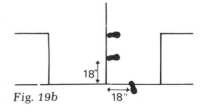

Fig. 19b

transfer. The wrist starts in the cocked position allowing a more powerful stroke. The wrist at the top of the backswing, keeps the racket vertical (or even sloping towards the front wall) so it is easier to play shots when close to the back wall. If you have a dropped wrist you will find it much more difficult to get behind the ball when it is driven to the back corner (see Fig. 20). Again, you may notice that there are many top players whose wrists are not cocked at the top of the backswing. However, as with the forehand, they move into a cocked position once the downswing has started. (Their backswing is nevertheless high.)

It is often helpful to start the downswing by pulling at the base of the racket (see Fig. 21a), and not

Fig. 20. Incorrect: a common fault often seen in recent converts from tennis

Fig. 21a

Fig. 21b. Incorrect

Fig. 22

Fig. 23a

Fig. 23b. Incorrect and
dangerous follow-through

by dropping the wrist (see Fig. 21b). The ball should be struck somewhere close to the plane vertical to the side wall which would pass through the inside of the right knee (see Fig. 22). The strings must 'follow the ball', that is, you must hit right through the ball with a full and safe follow-through (see Fig. 23a)—an indicator of a technically correct swing.

SUMMARY

* As in the forehand, a high back-swing is required, with right shoulder lower than the left, to generate racket-head speed.
* Start the downswing by pulling at the base of the handle, *not* by dropping the wrist.
* To hit the ball hard, the body weight must not be moving in the opposite direction to which the ball is struck.
* Finish high.

4. The Drop Shot

There are basically two kinds of drop shots, called the 'Pakistani' and 'Egyptian' drop shots. The Pakistani drop is heavily cut whilst the Egyptian drop is floated. The pushed or floated drop is easier to control, but at a cost of being more predictable. Many players tend to float most of their drops on the one side and cut it on the other (ideally you should be able to cut and float drops on both sides of the court): that is they might cut their backhand drop and generally float the forehand drop shot. To a large degree, the more biased the grip is, the more this asymmetry is emphasized. For example, a player whose 'V' is well over to the left, and who shows four knuckles (see Chapter 1: The Grip), is likely to float the backhand drop and cut the forehand drop. These tendencies stem from the natural hitting positions with a biased grip. Experiment yourself with biased grips to see what I mean.

Whether floating or cutting the short shots, there is one very important principle and that is not to change the racket-head angle relative to the front wall in the impact area. This applies to even heavily cut drop shots.

Obviously the more closely the preparation resembles the backswing for the drive (particularly), lob and boast, the more deceptive the shot is likely to be (see Chapter 11: Deception). Some deception is often vital when playing short as, if the intention to play a drop shot is revealed, the opponent will move in swiftly and could well kill the ball. Naturally if he is too tired to move forward, or if he is desperately trying to recover from one of the back corners, the need for disguise is greatly reduced (see Chapter 10: Shot Patterns).

COMBINATION OF PAKISTANI BACKHAND AND EGYPTIAN FOREHAND DROP

Start on the backhand. Footwork is important, as balance is vital when executing a delicate shot. So begin with the right leg leading with 'toe-toe-corner' in a straight line (see Fig. 24). The advantage of the heavily cut drop is that the backswing can be very full and the whole action telegraphs power, yet the result is a heavily chopped

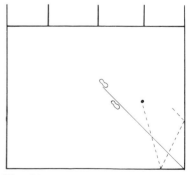

Fig. 24

ball dying in the forecourt (see Fig. 25). The cut on the ball does have some impact on its bounce, but I am convinced that its importance lies rather in the deception.

Fig. 25c

Whatever drop one employs, it is most important that the ball first hits the front wall and then the side wall. Ideally the ball falls into the nick (the join between the side wall and the floor) but it should never hit front wall, floor, side wall as the ball will 'sit up' inviting an easy kill.

The Egyptian floated drop is a delicate, but deadly, shot (see Fig. 26). The ball is brushed (so that it appears to roll off the racket) to float above the tin and, ideally,

Fig. 25a

Fig. 25b

Fig. 26

into the nick. The ball should strike the front wall after it has begun its downwards trajectory.

It needs to be mentioned that many of the Pakistanis, who float the forehand drop when the ball is close to the floor, have a pronounced cutting action to control the forehand drop as the ball bounces around knee-height and above.

CROSS-COURT DROP SHOTS

To hit a disguised cross-court drop, very little changes other than that you make contact with the ball slightly closer to the front wall. The footwork remains 'toe-toe-corner', the backswing and technique chosen remains the same, the impact is merely earlier. (See also Chapter 10: Shot Patterns. The cross-court drop is played ideally when the opponent has committed himself to covering the straight drop and he is moving too fast to change direction, and obviously when he does not expect the shot to be played to the front of the court.)

SUMMARY

* There are two types of drop shot: the Pakistani (cut) and the Egyptian (floated).
* The more common combination is the cut backhand and floated forehand drop. With a centred grip it is advisable to experiment first with this combination. The best international players will be able to cut and float on both sides.
* The heavily cut drop shot, because the preparation more closely resembles the preparation for the powerful drive, is probably the more deceptive type of drop.
* The deadly floated Egyptian drop, however, can move an opponent remorselessly as, if it is struck well, it dies so very close to the tin. It too can have an element of deception if it is played in combination with lobs having similar preparation.
* The drop shot must *not* hit front wall, floor, side wall.

5. The Lob

'The offense, you see, is play. The defense is work.... Offense is unrehearsed, exuberant, free-wheeling. Offense is an excitement which provides its own incitement. Its own compulsion. Its own driving force. It generates its own energy....

'Defense is dull, boring, common-place. It is the unimaginative plodding attention to duty. It is grit and determination and perseverance. It requires simply an act of the will. There is never a day you can't play defense. All you need is the decision to put out. To give one hundred percent.' (G. A. Sheehan)

The lob is probably the most under-utilized shot in a *complete* player's repertoire of shots, although it can be hit from both attacking and defensive positions. From an attacking position the lob can be employed to bury the opponent in a back corner with a minimum of energy expended in powering the ball. It is an excellent way of creating opportunities for really moving the opponent after his weak return, or for killing the ball. When employed from a defensive position, that is when you yourself are being worked or being 'yoyoed' around, the lob is the classic response as it buys you the all important time to recover the 'T'.

We shall consider both the lob played while balanced and the

shot played at full stretch. The end results should be the same—that the ball flies out of the opponent's reach and dies triumphantly in the corner. The techniques for lobbing cross-court and down the wall are the same.

Up to now consideration has been given only to 'correct' footwork. That is, playing the forehand and backhand in the classical positions: left foot leading for the forehand and right foot for the

Fig. 27a

Fig. 27b

backhand. The position of the feet when the lob is played is not vital for two reasons: firstly, leading with the wrong foot does give you added reach on the forehand (see Fig. 27); secondly, power is not required.

FROM THE BALANCED POSITION

The most important thing to remember is to hit up and through the ball, as height is essential to force the opponent right into the back corner. If the preparation for the lob is similar to that for your drop, the effect of the lob is that much more telling as you should have committed your opponent to covering the front of the court. He has thus to whirl around and chase towards the back corner (see also Chapter 11: Deception).

FROM THE STRETCHED POSITION

It is of primary importance when defending to make a good return. That is, the lob which goes 2.5 cm (1 in) out of court is totally useless. Obviously, to get the opponent on the whip-end with a beautifully tossed ball is the ideal, but the ball must not go out—particularly if you are out-of-hand (i.e. not serving). When fully stretched, it may be difficult to generate sufficient racket-head speed to propel the ball upwards to the back of the court. To overcome this, the racket should be swung in such a way that the open-faced racket-head approaches the ball from outside its line of flight (see Fig. 28). At impact, the ball is struck upwards with a flick of the wrist.

SUMMARY

* The lob is the outstanding shot for the harried player because he can thus buy himself time to recover the 'T' position and repay the oxygen debt (in layman's terms: recover his breath).
* The lob is a formidable attacking weapon to open up the court as the length ball is hit with little energy and the opponent's rhythm of play is often broken by shots of varying pace, particularly by the tantalizing lob. Moreover, with the exception of the very best in the world, most players are weak overhead.
* Hit up and through the ball, as height is of the essence in both defence and attack.

6. The Volley

The volley plays a vital role in modern squash. There are four basic reasons for this fact:

1. 'Pace' can be created not only by hitting the ball hard but also by volleying. It means a reduction in the time allowed the opponent before he launches himself towards his next stroke. The less time he has to rest between shots, the more severe the attrition is upon his body—he will be less able to recover his breath. Moreover, forcing the unfortunate opponent to rush between strokes makes it difficult for him to settle into any sort of rhythm of movement and stroke production.

2. In taking the ball early whilst the opponent is away from the 'T', one can afford to attack the forecourt more frequently (see Chapter 10: Shot Patterns).

3. A volley can prevent one's burial in the back court where stroke production is complicated by the back and side walls.

4. 'Hunting' the early ball ensures that where possible, the ball is struck with the body weight moving forward. Thus the potential for variations in pace is increased as an efficient weight transfer facilitates powerful shots.

The negative side of volleying is the fact that striking the ball early generally implies speedy movement with a high energy cost. Therefore, to play a modern attacking game, the necessity for a well-conditioned body is paramount.

One general observation about volleying that is well worth making is that, as you strive to take the ball early, there is less time for elaborate shot preparation. Therefore the backswing should be restricted and the shot production kept as simple as possible. Remember you are creating pace by taking the ball early. In most cases it is unnecessary to hit the ball at 100 m.p.h.

The ball can obviously be volleyed from almost any position. I have chosen to deal briefly with the volley around shoulder level and the overhead because, when the ball is lower than shoulder level, the technique employed to hit the ball is similar to that used when the ball has bounced.

VOLLEY AROUND SHOULDER LEVEL

I find it is useful to tell pupils to hit the ball in this position with a 'karate chop' action or with the outside edge of the racket leading (see Fig. 29). With this action a certain amount of chop and side spin is imparted to the ball. This will help bring the ball down in the corners. This technique is one which will give good controlled placements (when practised!) rather than tremendous pace.

Fig. 29a

Fig. 29b

THE OVERHEAD

Probably the area of maximum difference between a good player and a world-class player lies in the abilities to control the overhead. It is an area in which we can all improve. Jonah Barrington has won many matches by exploiting his opponents' weakness overhead. This tactic, complemented by an incredibly fit body and a very strong mind, led to six British Open titles. The British Open is regarded as the premier event in squash. I well remember the final in 1972 at Abbeydale when Jonah beat Geoff Hunt 3–2. Jonah lobbed so very well to show eventually that Geoff was not invincible.

The simplest method of hitting the overhead is to swing from the inside out, or, in other words, with the outer edge of the racket leading. The technique on the forehand is very similar to that employed in the tennis serve (see Fig. 30). If the ball is to be hit short, it must be struck *in front of the body*.

Fig. 30

DECEPTION AND THE EXCEPTIONAL

Good control and deception can be achieved with an outside-in swing. The deception comes from the fact that, as the player is swinging with the inside edge of the racket leading, the opponent expects the ball to go cross-court (following the racket-head arc), whereas the ball, in fact, goes down the wall. On the backhand side the wrist is, in fact, broken or dropped. This backhand stroke is probably easier to play with a grip which is slightly biased to the left (see Fig. 31).

Cam Nancarrow, who has an uncanny ability to hit the nick, employs both techniques when striking the ball overhead. That is, he can swing at the ball from both inside and outside the arc of the ball's flight.

Fig. 31

SUMMARY

* The volley is vital to create pace, to force openings and to exploit openings.
* Generally, a short backswing when volleying is necessary to ensure an accurate placement.
* Control on the volley around shoulder level is achieved using a 'karate chop' action.
* The simplest method for hitting the overhead is with the outside edge of the racket leading or, put another way, swinging from inside outwards.
* If the placement is to be made in the front of the court the ball must be struck in front of the body.
* The ambitious club player might experiment with hitting the overhead swinging from the outside in and thus improving his powers to deceive.

7. Angles

The angle is a shot which strikes the side wall nearest the striker before travelling to the front wall. The angle is sometimes called a boast or side-wall shot.

The boast generally is an easier shot to control than the drop shot. This does not make the boast a superior shot to the drop as, because the ball travels a longer distance when boasted (it must first hit the side wall), there is that fraction more time for an opponent to leap on to the loose boast and kill it. Moreover, a tight, straight drop presents the opponent with decisions as to whether or not he can afford a new racket!

As long as the boast is played once the opponent's position and direction of movement has been considered, it is an invaluable shot to send him to the front of the court. Possibly the word 'considered' is inappropriate, rather you should *develop an awareness* of the opponent's movements. Given the fact that the boast is easier to control, it should be played when the straight drop is considered too risky to attempt and yet the situation is such that it is safe to send the opponent to the front of the court.

Anyone who has watched Gogi Alauddin remorselessly tire his foe with cunningly placed drops, lobs and boasts, will not doubt the potential effectiveness of the boast. It should be noted, however, that Gogi covers the short balls he plays. That is, he is almost always balanced and poised on the 'T', even moving forward, when his opponent strikes the ball. Moreover, Gogi possesses cat-like agility and speed on court and can attempt shot patterns lesser mortals are advised not to try. (See Chapter 9: Movement and Chapter 10: Shot Patterns.)

Before we look briefly at the different types of boast, it is worth starting out with an observation and a warning. The observation is that players who hit a hard attacking boast well, tend to hit upwards and through the ball (the ball being reasonably close to the floor) with a slightly closed face. The technique for the attacking boast should be as similar to the technique employed for the drive as possible, the only difference being that the ball is contacted fractionally earlier in the swing.

As with most simple rules or observations this does need to be

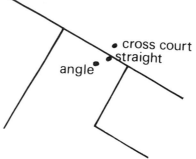

Fig. 32. Illustrating contact points

qualified by saying that many players do cut their boast to make it die earlier. The undercut action is also useful for taking the pace off the ball. As with the drop shot, many players tend to hit a flatter angle, even slightly topspun, on one side while cutting the ball more sharply on the other side.

The warning is that players can make errors by pulling away from the direction of the stroke (see Fig. 33). You should strive always to move your body weight in the direction in which the ball is struck. Admittedly the ball going in the direction opposite to that of the body movement is deceptive, but this ploy should be well practised before being implemented in a match. (See Chapter 11: Deception.)

Fig. 33a

SIX CATEGORIES OF ANGLES

1. Three-wall boast

The ball is played to hit the third wall simultaneously with the floor, that is to die in the nick. The shot is normally played from the back of the court. (If you are in the front of the court you are likely to hit a more direct kill.) To hit the three-wall boast, the ball is struck to make approximately a 45° angle with the side wall. This boast can be struck hard and low if the striker is well balanced, but it can also be floated across the court. This ensures that the striker has enough time to regain the 'T' should his shot miss the nick. The three-wall boast should always be struck to hit the third wall before the floor—the optimum being that it falls into the nick. If it strikes the floor before the third wall, the opponent is often presented with an easy kill.

This shot should be used with much caution against a fresh and fast opponent, but can be used with increasing disdain as the attrition tells on the opposition's

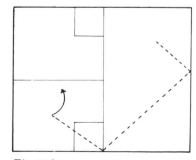

Fig. 33b

movements and co-ordination. If you intend experimenting with the three-wall boast, it is worthwhile noting that your opponent is more likely to return the shot across the court than down the wall. This is because it is easier to hit a ball, coming at you from the side wall and nearly parallel to the front wall, across the court. Thus you should position yourself more across the court, at least level with the 'T' (see Fig. 34).

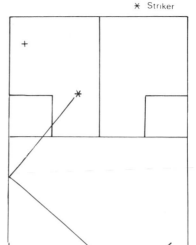

Fig. 35

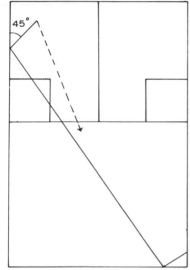

Fig. 34

2. **Hard boast**

Ken Hiscoe is a famous exponent of the attacking, hard-hit angle—struck to die second bounce in the nick or in the front of the court well away from the opponent (see Fig. 35). One of the advantages of this type of angle is that it does not have as far to travel as the three-wall boast. This shot, as with all shots, is that much more effective when struck on the volley.

3. **Float boast**

The name 'float boast' aptly describes the shot. The ball should be well on its downward trajectory when it strikes the front wall. Because the ball travels slowly towards its destination in the front of the court, an awareness of your opponent is vital. The float boast, being such a delicate stroke, should be played only when the striker is well balanced.

4. **Trickle or fiddle boast**

This shot is played in the front of the court. Because of this and as the ball ends up away from the side wall, it is necessary for the opponent to be well out of position, or deceived as to the nature of the shot.

One of the best ways of deceiving the opponent is with the aid of a full backswing designed to trick

37

him into reacting by moving backwards on to his heels. Another ploy is to show a drop shot and to turn it into a fiddle boast. To be successful the striker must have the opponent rushing in to cover the straight shot and be moving at such a committed pace to be unable to cope with the angle. In these circumstances, however, the safer shot to play would be the lob.

A useful tip when playing the trickle boast, whilst showing a straight drive, is to hit the ball to make contact with the side wall close to the front wall (see Fig. 36).

straight drop. (The former tactic is often skilfully practised by Yasin, a great Pakistani stroke player.) If the attempt to deceive misfires, the opponent has the complication of a side wall to contend with and, if straight length is hit, the striker has more time to recover a central position. (See Chapter 11: Deception.)

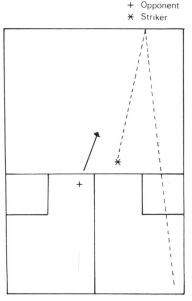

Fig. 37

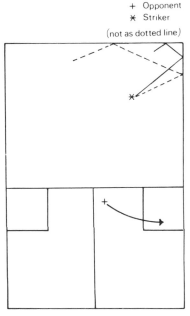

Fig. 36

In this way the ball starts out and is hit in much the same way as you wish the opponent to perceive it.

Whilst on the topic of deception it is appropriate to mention that it is better to show a boast and to hit down the wall to length or to hit a

Another trick, possibly best used by Asran (a talented Egyptian player), is to hit a heavily top-spun straight drop. Most opponents will run for an angle. Try it and see why.

5. Skid boast

The skid, or lob, boast is a handy shot played to relieve pressure. The opponent is often most disconcerted to find you have returned the ball deep into the opposite back corner (see Fig. 38)

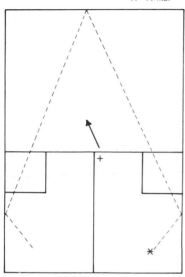

Fig. 38

when he was certain he had forced a weak boast from you. The ball is played firmly with an open racket face and hit upwards high on to the side wall. The actual angle to the side wall depends on your position, but once the shot has been practised you soon develop a feel for the angle.

The shot is really effective when the side walls are smooth and fast, as the ball can be sent readily into the opposite back corner. On a slow, cold court this shot must be used with discretion as it could give an easy kill position to the opponent. Still, if you are really under pressure, you at least force the opponent to *hit* the winner. Moreover, by its very nature the shot gives you time to recover a central position and thus you have a better chance to retrieve the next stroke.

6. Squeeze boast

The squeeze boast is a boast off a ball clinging to the side wall. This shot is very definitely to be left to top players otherwise the racket manufacturers will retire as millionaires! As far as I know, this innovation is attributed to Abu Taleb, the great Egyptian wizard with a racket. The ball is squeezed off the side wall with a most unusual technique probably best illustrated by a series of photographs (see Figs. 39a, b and c on next page). These show the forehand action. The inside edge of the racket leads and the ball is squeezed off the wall into a boast. The wrist is loose and dropped. The racket is loosely held. The same comments apply on the backhand.

This shot may be practised by dropping the ball vertically down the side wall and then attempting the stroke. Initially you will find you may hit the ball twice, but with practice your percentage of successful squeezed boasts improves enormously. It is respectfully suggested that the practice routine is embarked upon with an old racket.

For the average player this clinging ball should be hit down the wall with a flicking action—it is *not* possible to hit the ball in the middle of the strings! Try to flick the ball *high* to a length. The necessity for height is increased because it is almost impossible to flick a real clinger consistently across the court, and thus a thinking opponent will be waiting for the predictable down-the-wall return. This fact naturally makes the squeezed boast a useful shot in your repertoire.

39

Fig. 39a

Fig. 39b

Fig. 39c

REVERSE ANGLES

A forehand which first hits the left-hand side wall, as you are facing the front wall, is termed a reverse angle. Likewise a backhand which strikes the right-hand side wall first is a reverse angle.

+ Opponent
* Striker

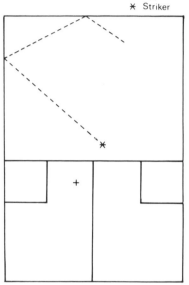

Fig. 40. The forehand reverse angle

An observation which springs immediately to mind is that beginners play the reverse angle far too often and the best players in the world (with the exception of Zaman and Safwat) seldom play it.

The danger of using the reverse angle stems from the fact that the ball travels a long way before dying in the front of the court. Thus, if the opponent is not deceived into believing that the ball was going cross-court, the opponent is presented with a bouncing ball in the front of the court.

The reverse angle is, however, an important weapon to be used when the match has been in progress some time and many 'ordinary' wide cross-court drives have been played. Most players will automatically move for the cross-court, as the execution of the reverse angle differs only fractionally from the drive across the court. But, to repeat, keep the reverse angle as a surprise weapon—use it sparingly!

I managed to beat Ken Hiscoe in the South African Open in 1977. During the course of the match I played a reverse angle and was surprised that Ken had committed himself so much to the cross-court drive. As a consequence I repeated the reverse angle a few more times during the match and must have hit four winners (at altitude where it is not easy to hit a winner). So it is not a bad idea to see how an opponent reacts to a reverse angle.

DEFENCE

The reverse angle can be used with some success when the striker is at *full* stretch in the front of the court. The striker would be unable to execute a lob but just manages to hit a high (preferably) reverse angle which ends up bouncing very close to the front wall. The opponent is generally able to hit a winner, but as the reverse angle was hit high, the striker has time to cover all but the best-attempted kills. Moreover, a high bouncing ball right in the front of the court can lead to an error from an over-excited opponent. This strategy, to repeat, is *only* to be used when it is not possible to lob the ball to the back.

BACK-WALL BOAST

The back-wall boast is a shot which first hits the back wall before travelling to the front wall. It is very much a shot of 'last resort' as the opponent is presented with a relatively easy kill. The back-wall boast is used when you have been well beaten by a good-length stroke and there is no other option open to you. The shot is played as if you were trying to hit a firm lob off the back wall. That is, if you have been beaten on the *forehand* side of the court, you might still be able to hit a *backhand* on to the back wall which will carry to the front wall (see Fig. 41). The key to making a good return is to hit upwards on to the back wall. You will be amazed at how little power is required to send the ball to the front wall.

Fig. 41

With practice it is possible to achieve a degree of control so that the shot finishes reasonably close to the side wall.

SUMMARY

* Try to integrate all five varieties of the angle into your game: the three-wall, hard, float, trickle and the skid boast. The squeeze boast is to be left to the top players. The greater the range of strokes at your command, the more difficult it is for your opponent to anticipate your next stroke and to get into a rhythm.

* As the first four types of boast mentioned above are played to the front of the court, the striker must have an awareness of his opponent. Once the enemy is sent to the front of the court, you must ensure you cover the front of the court. That is, you must be on the 'T' and have forward momentum. (See Chapter 9: Movement.)

* When playing the boast to the front of the court, unless the opponent is well out of position, it is necessary that the shot be disguised.

* The reverse angle is a good surprise tactic to use when the opponent is conditioned to the cross-court drive. It can also be used when desperate to keep the rally going and you are not able to achieve enough height on the lob from the front court.

* The back-wall boast is a 'last resort' shot—to be used when it is impossible to play any other stroke. It is important to hit upwards on to the back wall so that the ball carries to the front wall.

8. The Serve

Talking about the serve is very much a restatement of the obvious. Yet the obvious is often forgotten in the effort to remember the myriad of details which we believe will greatly improve our games.

The serve starts the rally and there is *absolutely no reason to start it sloppily*. Let us consider the serve from the receiver's position: what is he trying to do? The receiver will strive to volley the serve and gain a commanding position on the 'T'. In this light the server's strategy is simple: he must make it as difficult as possible for a receiver to volley and to move efficiently and economically to the 'T'.

A *fundamental principle* in squash is: if you find something difficult, so does your opponent. You find it awkward volleying very high balls, balls that are very close to the side walls, balls that have just bounced off the side wall, and balls coming at you from an unexpected angle. So does your opponent! Consider then how to thwart the enemy's objective with this knowledge in mind.

LOB SERVE

The lob serve is possibly the most obvious serve. The ball is tossed high on to the front wall to hit the side wall just below the red line and to pass away peacefully in the back court. A good lob serve is most difficult to volley and the opponent is forced to attempt to gouge the ball out of the back corners. The server, poised expectantly on the 'T', is ready for the weak return. With practice, very few mistakes need be made on this serve. However, practice is necessary.

ANGLE AND PACE

Many fine players choose not to lob their serve, as they are fearful of error, but rather hit the serve so that the receiver has to volley it very close to the side wall (preferably after the ball has hit the side wall). It is even better if the receiver allows the ball to go through to the back of the court. The pace of the serve may vary, in fact it should vary, and the serve may be struck overhead or from below the waist. However the serve is struck, it is often a good idea to serve backhand from the right box. Conversely it is a good idea to serve forehand out of the left box (see Fig. 42).

In this way the angle the ball makes with the side wall is minimized, particularly if the server leans well out of the box towards the 'T'. The pace of the serve is determined by the height of the serve and by the desire to hit a good length.

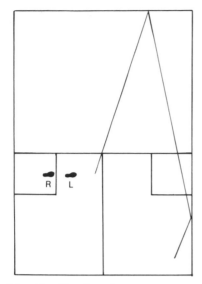

Fig. 42a. Forehand serve

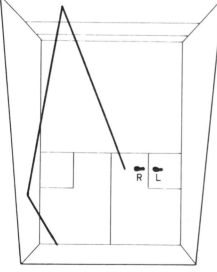

Fig. 42b. Backhand serve

MIDDLE OF THE ROAD

The unexpected hard serve down the middle of the court can turn out into an unexpected winner. I recall seeing Doug Barrow, probably one of the best squash players South Africa has produced, hitting John Easter on the head in this fashion. Doug tried not to laugh out aloud and John was not his usual dignified self. But what an easy point!

CORKSCREW

Another type of serve that can give the receiver problems is the corkscrew serve. The server stretches as far to the centre as possible before hitting the ball high and hard to the front wall about 30 cm (12 in) below the top red line to rebound approximately 30 cm (12 in) along the side wall. As the server has reached to the 'T' before serving, the ball will hit the side wall and rebound right across the court, hitting the opposite side wall near the back wall. The spin imparted to the ball from its front wall/side wall impact causes the ball to bounce out vertically from the side wall (nearest to the receiver—see Fig. 43).

To achieve the requisite depth the corkscrew serve should only be attempted on hot courts or in altitude conditions. This serve must be practised before being used in a match, and should only be attempted when the server is comfortably in command of the game as the margin of error is considerably smaller than on the conventional serve.

Incidentally, the corkscrew is a most spectacular kill to be played when presented with a bouncing ball in the front centre of the court. Again, because the margin of error is small and possibly because it is an unnecessarily elaborate kill, I

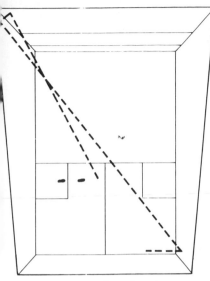

Fig. 43a. Forehand corkscrew serve

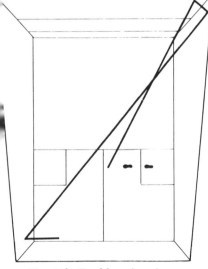

Fig. 43b. Backhand corkscrew serve

have not seen this shot attempted in really top squash. When presented with this sort of opening, the top players generally will hit the ball straight at the nick.

SUMMARY

* Play must be started in as constructive (or as destructive to the opponent) a way as possible.
* The classic return of serve is the volley down the wall to length. A fundamental principle to be borne in mind is: if you find something difficult, so does everyone else.
* To complicate or frustrate the attempt to volley the serve, use height, pace, placement of the ball uncomfortably close to the wall, or present the receiver with a ball coming at an unexpected angle. It is considered a golden rule when serving that the ball must always hit the side wall, the exception being when the serve is deliberately struck down the middle of the court.
* The height, angle and pace of the serve should be constantly varied. It is often useful to serve backhand as well as forehand in achieving this objective.
* The corkscrew serve should be attempted only after it has been mastered in practice and when the server is in command of the game.

Part II

Movement
Shot Patterns
Deception

An Introductory Note

Squash is an intensely physical game. Without a sensible game plan, you (as opposed to your opponent) are in danger of getting all the exercise! Even at the risk of repetition, it is important to have a sound idea of basic strategy before studying movement, shot patterns and deception.

The 'T' is the best position on the court—more accurately, a couple of feet behind the 'T'. From there you are best able to reach balls in any one of the corners and to volley many of your opponent's strokes. (See Chapter 6: The Volley.) The fundamental idea in this human game of chess is to dominate the 'T' and force your opponent out of good position. Once this has been achieved, placements (not necessarily winners) should be made, so that the opponent has to run many diagonals. The ultimate game, then, being one rally terminated not by a winner but by physical collapse!

Deceptive strokes can accelerate the physical demise of your opponent. He will move initially in the wrong direction and will then have to dart further and faster to retrieve the stroke. Further inroads into the opponent's well-being may also be made by ensur-ing that the preparation for each shot or for a combination of shots is similar—for example, for a lob and a drop or for a boast and a drive. This ability will ensure that the opponent is less able to move smoothly in anticipation of your next stroke because he is conscious of the threat of another shot.

In the unhappy event of your being raced around by your opponent, the obvious strategy is to strive to minimize your range and speed of movement by limiting your opponent's options and by regaining the 'T' before he is able to play his next shot. This is best done by returning the ball deep into the back of the court. If the return is lobbed into a back corner, the striker has more time to regain the 'T'. With the ball in the back of the court, the opponent is less likely to attack the forecourt owing to the possibility of error. The tighter the shot, in the sense of it being close to the side wall or else dying in the back corner, the more predictable is the opponent's stroke. And roles can then be reversed.

Bearing all this in mind, we move on to consider movement, shot patterns and deception.

9. Movement

'I am quite certain, however, that the Ultimate Athlete is a dancer.' (J. A. Michener)

'He is such a beautiful mover' is *not* often said of a squash player, but when it is, what exactly does it mean? Does it mean that the player moves at breath-taking speed, that he moves fluidly without exhausting stops and starts, that he always seems to have time, or merely that he plays the ball with the correct foot leading?

Probably it means most of these attributes, but how does a player go about improving them in his own game if he is not a 'beautiful mover'?

Before attempting to answer these questions, it is necessary to state (the obvious, perhaps) that a player is best able to attack *and* defend from the central 'T' position. Thus a player must always strive to regain the 'T' once he has played his shot.

SPEED

Your speed can be improved markedly by what is appropriately called speed training and by improved flexibility.

1. Speed training

Speed training involves repeating the specific movement flat-out for about five to thirty seconds. You rest in between sets, it is best to walk around, until your pulse is about 100 beats per minute. Repeat this schedule a total of perhaps four to ten times.

I have been vague in specifying the duration of effort, the interval and the number of sets to be completed. This is deliberate as with speed training the emphasis is very much upon *quality*. It is better to do fewer repetitions of the movement, recover for longer periods and thus be able to move flat-out in each set. See Chapter 13 where speed work is covered in depth.

Speed training can only accomplish its goal when the body is already fit and strong. A person who has led a relatively sedentary existence must first do much mileage at a slower pace to build up the stamina before attempting to improve his speed.

2. Flexibility

A second attribute which will improve effective speed is greater flexibility. The importance of flexibility cannot be over-emphasized—there is a more detailed exposition, including the Yoga-type positions to be held, in Chapter 15. Improved flexibility not only increases your effective speed, it helps prevent injuries and it is reported to aid recovery from strenuous physical exertion.

AVOIDANCE OF EXHAUSTING STOPS AND STARTS

The key to good movement lies in avoiding the static position. That is, where possible, maintain a forward momentum. This is particularly important when your opponent is in the front of the court, as the most dangerous shots to cover are the short shots. If he lobs or hits to length, you are going to have to wheel around mighty smartly to retrieve, but, because the ball has to travel further (to the back of the court), you have that much more time to recover. Try to get to a drop shot from a static or stationary position on the 'T'—it is very, very difficult!

Even when the opponent is in the back of the court, your momentum should still be slightly forward—after all, even if he is trying to hit to length, you are always hunting the volley. With your opponent behind you, you may find yourself in a static position. In this case it is preferable that your weight is mostly on your rear foot, and in the process of being transferred when your opponent strikes the ball. If you

also go down, that is bend your knees, as your opponent hits his shot, you will find yourself better prepared to spring away towards the ball.

Notice from Fig. 44 that I am watching my opponent as he is about to strike the ball. It is important to turn to watch your opponent as the open movement to the front of the court (the area furthest from the 'T') from this position, is the most efficient. But more important is the fact that, in facing your opponent, you avoid the shortcomings of the proverbial 'front-wall watcher' who only reacts when the ball enters his periphery vision.

Fig. 45

The player who turns and watches is able to receive signals of his opponent's intentions earlier than the front-wall watcher. With experience comes the ability to interpret more accurately the opponent's exact intentions from these signals. It is often

Fig. 44

51

not possible to watch the ball leaving the racket (as it has been hit too hard) but the player will have registered many other facts from turning and watching. For example, he may note that the opponent is so stretched, that anything but a boast is unlikely. On top of this, by watching the opponent he will pick up the ball earlier than the front-wall watcher.

The player who reacts earlier has more time for efficient and economical movement and is better able to deceive. He can, for example, pause momentarily at the top of the backswing and cause his opponent to assume a static position on the 'T'. And it is the stopping, twisting and starting which saps the opponent's store of energy.

CORRECT FOOTWORK

When writing this book I approached a professional photographer to get some action shots. He apologized that he had few action shots played from the clas-

sical positions—most were off the 'wrong' foot (see Fig. 46). This could support a few hypotheses: that the top players and coaches are having us on; that they have perfected an error; that there is no one correct way of hitting a ball and that results alone count; or even that there are good reasons for playing off the 'wrong' foot.

My advice is that you should practise (see Chapter 14: Training with the Ball) in the classical position 65 per cent of the time. This of course implies you must practise playing off the 'wrong' foot. Remember, you can stretch further when playing forehands off the 'wrong' foot; and when lobbing or floating the ball, your control is probably much the same whether playing 'correctly' or not. When playing off the 'wrong' foot, a skilled player is still able to generate racket-head speed by turning his shoulders.

The classical position, on balance, does seem to give a greater potential for a wider range of strokes. In particular, the classical position facilitates shoulder and hip turn and the transfer of weight—this increases the range of pace at which the ball may be struck.

FOOTWORK WHEN PLAYING FROM THE BACK CORNERS

1. Forehand

When forced to play the ball after it has hit the back wall in the corner, your first step into the corner should be with your right leg, so that your right foot is closer to the back wall. This is best

Fig. 46

explained visually (see Fig. 47) and in a series of steps.

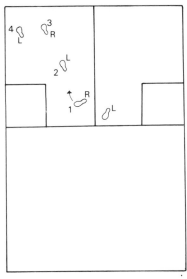

Fig. 47. Movement from 'T' to forehand corner

Step 1: Swivel right foot towards corner
Step 2: Left leg towards corner

Fig. 48

Step 3: Step into corner area with right foot
Step 4: Left leg as indicated, so that you are facing into the corner

This footwork will facilitate your weight transfer and will improve your ability to cope with a ball that bounces awkwardly out of the corner.

2. **Backhand**

This is clearly illustrated in Fig. 49. You will notice that the left leg is closer to the back wall, and that both legs are well spread to give good balance.

Fig. 49

PRACTICE FROM THE BACK CORNERS

1. Forehand

Hold the ball against the back wall near the corner with your left hand at shoulder-height. Position your feet as illustrated in Fig. 47 and have the racket at the top of the backswing as in Fig. 48. From this position throw the ball down past your left foot and strike it such that it returns to you down the wall. Once you have accomplished this, throw the ball progressively closer and closer to the back wall until such time as you are forced to boast to make a good return. You may find that you can delay having to use the boast in this exercise if you swing so that the racket arc is more around the body and if, just prior to contacting the ball, you stop the base of the racket-grip, thus enabling the head to come around more sharply.

2. Backhand

The same procedure is followed to practise playing the backhand from the back corner. This time, however, start by throwing the ball past the right foot. You will also be able to establish at what stage you will have to use the side wall to assist you in making a good return.

STARTING POSITION

1. Return of service

As mentioned in the chapter on the serve, the receiver should generally try to volley the serve to length. Given this objective the player should position himself as in Fig. 50 when receiving serve. If, from this position, you move forward and volley to length, you are entitled to move straight to the 'T'.

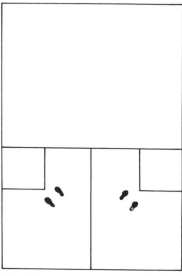

Fig. 50

If you are forced to play the ball from the back corner to length, your movement will be as in Fig. 51—as you have to give your opponent direct access to the ball. Your movement towards the 'T' is obviously now more difficult than if you had volleyed the serve to length and moved directly to the 'T' (see Fig. 52).

Mike Corby, the great British coach, always tells his pupils, when jostling for the 'T' in the course of a rally of length shots, to 'hit the ball and walk *forward*' (see Fig. 53). This is very sound advice, but to do this you must be confident in your ability to hit good length. Should you mis-hit the ball mid-court and walk forward, you will be penalized in a match.

+ Opponent
* Striker

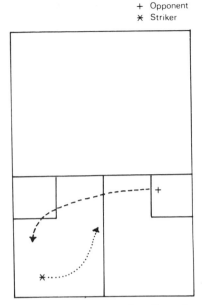

Fig. 51. Movement when forced into the corner and returning the ball down the wall

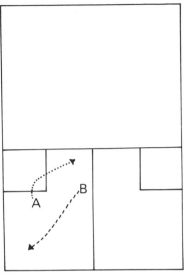

Fig. 53. A and B jostling for the dominating position. A hits the ball and walks forward. He is now in front

+ Opponent
* Striker

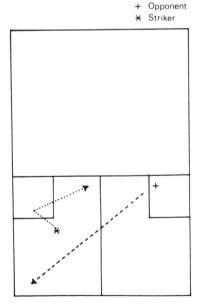

Fig. 52

2. Service

When we discussed the serve, we mentioned how the angle the ball makes with the side wall could and should be varied. But from which part of the box should you serve? You only have to have one foot completely grounded within the box to avoid being foot-faulted.

Most players serve from the middle of the box and move directly across the court towards the centre. Many good players move slightly backwards (from the front wall) after the serve, on the not unreasonable assumption that the receiver will play the ball to length. (See Chapter 10: Shot Patterns.) Given the importance of forward momentum discussed above, it is advisable that you do

55

not move backwards. There is, however, an exception: namely, when you serve from the front of the box to get maximum height on your lob serve. If you serve further forward you are able to hit the ball higher (see Fig. 54).

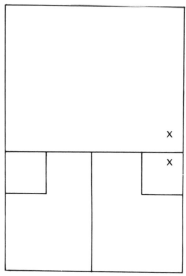

Fig. 54a

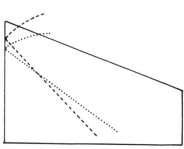

Fig. 54b

From this serve you can move backwards towards a commanding position, but then you must be prepared to spring forward to pounce upon a weak return.

RACKET UP OR DOWN?

It makes sound sense that, when receiving serve or during a rally, you wait (with forward momentum!) for the ball with your racket up. This will save you having to lift the racket when the ball comes towards you, thus preventing a rushed backswing. When feasible then, begin movement towards the ball at the same time as drawing the racket back. (It is obviously not sensible to move in this fashion when attempting to scrape up a good drop.)

You may have noted that a few good players do arrive on the 'T' with the racket down. Nevertheless, almost all the top players do prepare early for their shots and have an early, unhurried backswing to ensure a fluid stroke (as Hunt illustrates in Fig. 55).

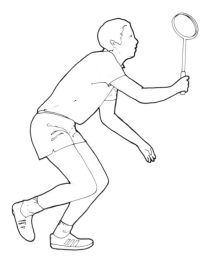

Fig. 55

To conclude, it is worthwhile experimenting with keeping the racket head up to see if it assists you in early preparation for your strokes.

SUMMARY

* Speed training—training of a very intense nature for a short duration of time—can markedly increase speed. Emphasis is to be on quality when considering intervals and repetitions. See detailed discussion in Chapter 13.
* Greater flexibility can often improve movement. See exercises in Chapter 15.
* When the opponent is in the front of the court, it is imperative to avoid a static position on the 'T'. You must be moving forward to cover the most dangerous shots.
* If you are in a crouched, bent-leg position as your opponent strikes the ball, you are more ready to spring powerfully away in pursuit thereof.
* When the opponent is behind you, you must have turned to watch him. Your weight must not be on your heels. It is a good idea to be moving slightly forward as he strikes the ball.
* Practise playing the ball off both feet on each side of the court. When possible, try to play off the 'correct' foot as this increases the range of strokes open to you. Note that, even going in on the 'wrong' foot, you can still turn the shoulders to generate racket speed if power is required.
* Playing off the 'wrong' foot may increase your reach, and your ability to control a floated shot is not diminished.
* Try to volley to length your opponent's serve and walk forward to gain command of the 'T'.
* Movement from the serve is geared to achieve a dominating position so that you are able, wherever possible, to go forward on attack.
* Prepare early for the shot. It is suggested that you receive serve and wait for subsequent shots with the racket head up.
* In the back corners, when forced to play the ball after it has struck the back wall, your footwork should be such that you play the ball facing into the corner.

10. Shot Patterns

An offensive must be built up by attacking the ball to length. Force the opponent to play the ball going backwards. Where possible, volley the ball to length. This is even more unsettling for the opponent, as he has less time to recover in between shots. In this way you will eventually force a weak return from the harassed man. Put another way, a weak return is inevitable from a player who has been well and truly buried in the back of the court. Once you are presented with a ball in the middle or front of the court, you can go about your business of moving your opponent or killing the ball—depending upon the nature of the opening.

GOLDEN RULE

A golden rule to be observed is not to give your opponent the front of the court for nothing. Your opponent must really work to gain this privilege! This follows from the fundamental principle of squash (slightly inverted): what you do well so do most others. Basically, everyone is good in the front of the court *when* they have time on their side. Hence it is vital to attack the front of the court only once you have outmanoeuvred your opponent and are confident you will not present him with an easy kill. Furthermore, when you do play short you must be in a position to cover any short shots he plays. (See Chapter 9: Movement.)

AWARENESS OF OPPONENT

Probably the most tiring movement on court is the movement to and from the front of the court. Thus you must play short but bear in mind the two conditions previously mentioned. Namely, avoid giving the opponent a balanced position in the forecourt and ensure that you cover the front so that you are able to pounce on the counter-drop or trickle boast. Three factors, primarily, determine his difficulty in reaching the ball: his position when the ball is struck; his direction of movement if he is not static; his speed of movement. Thus an awareness of the opponent is necessary if he is to be sent scurrying forward without endangering your offensive momentum. Not only is this awareness vital for hitting the ball short, but it will improve your pattern and choice of all shots.

Below are a few scenarios drawn up to illustrate the points made above. A and B are two players.

Scenario 1

If A is forced to hit a back-wall boast it is *generally* safe for B to drop the ball if B moves rapidly to the shot. If, however, B hears A thundering up, his correct reply is the lob. This ensures that A does not volley as he is rushing to the front of the court.

Scenario 2

In the fifth game, A notices B has slowed up markedly and is tending to hang back from the 'T'. A consequently becomes more adventurous and hits more boasts and drops, but at the same time ensuring that he covers the short balls.

Scenario 3

B has just hit a weak cross-court drive from the front of the court and is back-pedalling very fast to the 'T'. A can use this opportunity to boast B back whence he is so rapidly coming.

Scenario 4

B plays a loose drive down the wall. A is quick to strike the ball across the court. This is an effective strategy as B is still turning to look at A and must now whirl around to the opposite back corner (see Fig. 56).

Scenario 5

A jumps swiftly out of the way of a ball he has mis-hit down the wall. He performs this spectacular evasive action to avoid a penalty point. B senses that the referee will not award him the point—perhaps the referee has been reluctant all through the match to award points. B, however, is sure that despite A's 'sporting' effort to clear the ball, he will be returning very rapidly to cover the down-the-wall drive (see Fig. 57). Given this, the

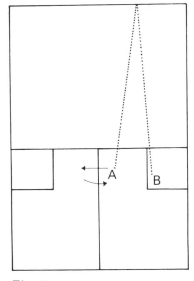

Fig. 56. An effective use of the cross-court

Fig. 57

sensible shot for B to play would be the boast, cross-court drive or drop. B, being an astute player, would probably hit the drive if he were hand-out, and the boast or drop if he were hand-in (see below).

It is possible to paint many other scenarios but these five should suffice. To reiterate, it is vital to develop an awareness of your opponent's position, direction and speed of movement.

HITTING ACROSS THE LINE OF MOVEMENT

I have chosen to isolate one particular strategy as it can be employed so effectively. Zaman is one top player who is very good at hitting across the line of movement. This idea is better explored in a diagram (see Fig. 58). Zaman has developed an uncanny feeling for his opponent's direction and

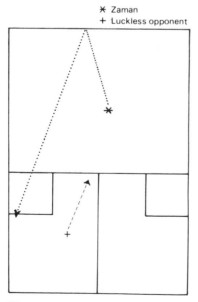

✳ Zaman
✛ Luckless opponent

speed of movement. He exhausts even very fit players in a relatively short space of time by making them dart, stop and twist continuously. That, as mentioned before, is the most effective way of tiring the opponent. However, Zaman sometimes goes to extremes and nearly kills them! (Note, however, that it would be senseless to play the shot as illustrated in Fig. 58 unless the opponent was moving *very* rapidly towards the 'T'.)

HAND-IN, HAND-OUT STRATEGIES

'Hand-in' merely implies you are serving, 'hand-out' that you are receiving serve. When you are hand-out, an error gives the opponent a point. In this light, to state that your shot pattern when hand-out should be more conservative, or rather geared to forcing an error from your opponent, seems slightly trite. Yet the two different strategies must be built into a player's reflex patterns. It is all too easy to forget you are hand-out as you wing the overhead towards the cross-court nick. What are your percentages? And what is the score? These factors have to play a role in determining your shot pattern, yet there is not time to think of them on court. It is only through *disciplined* practice games that reflexes are conditioned to play the correct sequence of strokes based upon an awareness of the opponent, the score and who is serving.

SUMMARY

* Build up your attack by hitting, preferably volleying, to length and then attacking, using the forecourt, the inevitably weak return.
* Make him earn the 'right' to play in the front of the court. Ensure that you cover the counter-drop and that he is unable to reach the ball in the forecourt perfectly balanced.
* Awareness of the opponent's position, direction and speed of movement is vital in deciding the next shot. This awareness is built up over time, but must be consciously developed.
* Hitting across the opponent's line of movement can be a very telling strategy if he is moving fast.
* Hand-out shot patterns must be more conservative than the hand-in pattern.

11. Deception

The ability to send an opponent in the wrong direction is a tremendous asset. If you can deceive your opponent, then the margin for error on your winning stroke can be that much greater. Even more important is the fact that, if the opponent starts out in the wrong direction, the energy cost of recovering the ball is very high.

TECHNIQUES USED

Often a combination of the factors mentioned below will be used to beguile the opponent. Setting these factors out in separate categories should aid you in integrating added variety and deception into your game.

Fig. 59

1. Wrist action

At the last moment, the use of a flexible wrist can be most helpful in sending the opponent the wrong way. The Pakistani players generally are skilled in this form of deception. A strong wrist, built up by many hours of hitting and exercises using weights, is an essential ingredient to this form of deception. A flexible wrist increases the range of the wrist movement and hence the potential to deceive. Flexibility of the wrist can be improved using Indian clubs or by consciously striving to increase the wrist's range of movements.

2. Delay

Very much allied to a strong and flexible wrist is the use of what is called 'delay'. A pause at the top of an early backswing may well get an opponent to assume a static position, or else to commit himself prematurely to cover the *anticipated* shot. If you notice the premature committal, ensure that the ball is dispatched in the opposite direction.

3. Hiding the ball and action

Skilfully hiding the ball and wrist action from the opponent's sight, using one's own body, will mean he is able to interpret fewer signals. As a result of this greater uncertainty he will more frequently assume static positions, and, as a consequence, will have to do a lot more work.

4. Body movement

Deliberate movement of the body, in a direction opposite to which the ball is struck, is often most deceptive. For example, when set up in the front forehand court, you hit the ball down the side wall simultaneously twisting and turning the body inwards towards the centre of the court (see Fig. 60).

Fig. 61

5. Racket arc

The arc of the racket can be instrumental in sending the opponent in the wrong direction.

Fig. 60

Similarly, it is deceptive to hit the ball across the court whilst rotating the head and shoulders towards the nearest side wall (see Fig. 61).

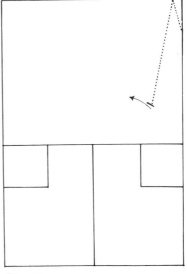

Fig. 62

If the racket is swung from the 'outside in', that is, across the line of the ball's flight, most players will expect the ball to travel across the court. If, however, the face of the racket is opened, the ball can be made to go straight relative to the side wall. This is best explained pictorially (see Fig. 62). The deception is derived from the fact that most often the strings follow the ball. In this case, the strings and the ball go in different directions.

6. Variation in shots

Although not strictly speaking a technique to improve or achieve deception, a wide variety of shots is most useful in creating a greater uncertainty in the opponent's mind and it is therefore part and parcel of the art of deception. You are more likely to get a flat-footed opponent reluctant to commit himself, if, when you come to play your sixth stroke from the same position on court, you have already played five completely different shots. Thus, the greater the variation in shots, the more easily the opponent will fall into the trap of assuming a static position.

Naturally the effect of greater variety is increased if the preparation for each shot is similar. Thus a drop shot hit from a full backswing is that much more effective than one that is jabbed, with little backswing, above the tin.

THREE OBSERVATIONS

In case the deception fails, it is probably better to hit the tight shot. For example, showing a boast and hitting a straight drop is preferable to showing the drop and hitting the boast. Another illustration of this point would be hitting the drive down the wall after showing a boast, rather than *vice versa*.

The second observation is that after employing deception with effect, *showing and hitting* the obvious shot can provide an easy winner. Once you have shown a subtle and deceptive shot pattern, the opponent is less willing to believe the signals you are giving when you telegraph a trickle boast with your body and shoulders pointing at the side wall. Thus the trickle boast itself is the most deceptive shot.

Finally, do not try to be too deceptive. Play the obvious winner to open-court when the opening is presented. An example of the moment to hit the obvious winner can be seen in Fig. 63. B should strike the obvious open-

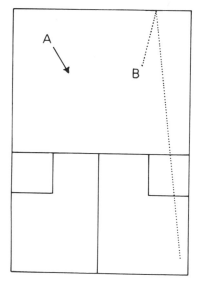

Fig. 63

court winner to length and not attempt to wrong-foot A. In these circumstances it is obviously the correct shot as A is so out of position—in other circumstances it is less obvious, especially when you are on court!

Certainly, try to wrong-foot your opponent, but the balance between this and moving him maximum distance must be carefully chosen. There is no short cut to this balance, but a thinking player will acquire it much sooner than the man who 'just has a good sweat'.

PRACTICE

Like all things in squash, deception has to be practised before being implemented in a match. Routines, both single and dual, to practice are covered in Chapter 14: Training with the Ball.

SUMMARY

* Probably the most effective method for deceiving the opponent is with a late wrist action.

A flexible wrist, that is one with a wide range of movement, better enables the ball to be struck in the direction which the opponent thought unlikely.
* Delaying your shot and hiding the ball from your opponent may also force your opponent to do more work.
* Body movement and racket arcs, in directions opposite to which the ball is struck, often mislead the opponent.
* A wide variety of strokes at hand, each with similar backswing, is part and parcel of the attempt to improve deception.
* Three observations:
1. *Hit* the tight shot where there is a choice in the manner in which deception is to be achieved.
2. Once you have deceived your opponent a few times and shown a subtle and full range of strokes, *showing and hitting* the shot can be the most effective strategy.
3. Try to establish the correct balance between attempts at deception and playing solid open-court shots to move the opponent maximum distances.

Part III

The Warm-up and Warm-down
Training without the Ball
Training with the Ball
Flexibility

12. The Warm-up and Warm-down

RATIONALE BEHIND THE WARM-UP

Little more can be done than quote a relevant passage from the *Squash Player* (March 1978, p. 16). Dr Craig Sharp states:

For every 1½ degree F rise in temperature, the metabolic rate of the muscle, that is the rate at which it can utilise its fuel, increases by 14 per cent. Furthermore, the rise in temperature causes the muscle cell itself to become less viscous, much as syrup becomes more 'runny' when heated in a saucepan. This enables the muscle to work with greater mechanical efficiency, and may partly be responsible for making the muscle less prone to injury.

Thus, these beneficial effects of internally generated muscle heat form part of the rationale behind a 'warm-up' routine before strenuous exercise—a routine which the vast majority of squash players (unlike athletes, gymnasts or dancers) ignore completely.

SCHEDULE

Below is a schedule, borrowed largely from Jonah Barrington and based upon a dancer's routine warm-up, which should be the minimum series of exercises run through by a player. Given Dr Sharp's advice, it is apparent that you should do *much* more than this simple schedule which is designed to loosen and stretch most of the ligaments, tendons and muscles in the body.

Ideally the player should have jogged some 800 to 1500 metres interspersed with intervals of fast running if he is to walk on court having built up a light sweat. It is useful just before a match to hit-up on a vacant court and to move through some typical squash movements. The actual knock-up period is then used to settle the nerves and to run through the gamut of strokes, particularly to length, on the match court.

Most players on circuit believe in a morning session of playing a game or two and doing a few drills when they have to play an important match in the evening. One always seems to play that much better in the second session of the day. Even having completed a morning session, these players will still warm-up prior to the big match.

Jonah Barrington's schedule is very similar to the following:

1. Foot tapping

Tap each foot at least ten times (see Fig. 64). This exercise is designed to improve the 'viscosity' of the achilles tendon. This exercise looks a bit feeble and you may be mocked for doing it, but if

Fig. 64

Fig. 66

you have seen the result of an achilles injury, you are completely inured to the mockery.

2. Rotation of ankle joint/toe circling

Rotate each foot in as large a circle as possible keeping the base of the heel stationary (see Fig. 65). Circle each foot ten times clockwise and ten times anti-clockwise.

Fig. 65

3. Alternate toe touch

With straight legs and feet about 1 m (39 in) apart, touch the left foot with the right hand (see Fig.

66), and then the right foot with the left hand. Repeat some thirty to forty movements. This exercise is particularly good in that it serves to 'lubricate' muscles in the leg, particularly the hamstring, the back and the shoulders.

4. Rotation of pelvis

With hands on the hips and legs apart, rotate the pelvis in a clockwise and then anti-clockwise direction (see Fig. 67). Do some

Fig. 67

ten circles or rather ellipses in each direction. The squash movement places a heavy stress upon the hip joint and it is vital to ensure this area has been well and truly 'warmed-up'.

5. **High kicking**

Supporting yourself with a rail or wall, swing your leg, keeping it straight, as high as you can and down again as far back as is comfortable, then swing it forward again (see Fig. 68). (The movement is continuous.) Repetitions depend, to a degree, upon how stiff you are, but I advocate at least twenty forward swings with each leg. This kicking, as with all the other exercises, should be done gently and smoothly. You progress slowly towards kicks to hip height and above.

6. **Forward lunges**

Position yourself as in Fig. 69 with feet about 1 m (39 in) apart. Apply gentle pressure to the inside of the thighs by lowering your body to the ground. You lower the body slightly in the direction of the bent knee by bending that knee more.

Fig. 68a

Fig. 68b

Fig. 69

Release the pressure, or rather the stretch, by raising your body weight. Repeat this pressure about fifteen times and then switch to the other leg in the leading position.

71

7. Lunges sideways

This exercise is done in much the same fashion as the forward lunge, the only difference being in the starting position. You will note from Fig. 70 that the shoulders, hips and legs are roughly in the same plane. The feet are slightly less than 1 m (39 in) apart. Repeat the pressure on each posture about fifteen times.

Fig. 71

Fig. 72

Fig. 70

8. Arms circling

Using straight arms, rotate them forwards so that they brush the ears and then the thighs. Do about twenty rotations forwards and then repeat circling the arms in the opposite direction (Fig 71).

9. Wrist movement

Grip the racket in the middle of the shaft and move the head of the racket to and fro between 'ten and two o'clock' (Fig 72).

10. Rotation of head

Rotate the head twice to the left and then twice to the right. More than this can cause dizziness.

Fig. 73

The above exercises are a suggested schedule. You may add, subtract and modify the exercises as you wish. But, to repeat, this schedule is the *absolute minimum* you should do before going on court. It is a good idea to run and to hit on a spare court before a match. If it is a practice session on court, it is good to begin with some routines (see Chapter 14).

INJURIES—A LAYMAN'S OPINION[1]

1. Consult a doctor who is experienced in sports medicine.
2. Do not rush into surgery—do absolutely everything else possible first.
3. Avoid, where possible, the short-term cure—for example the cortisone injection into the damaged area.[2] It is *not* the end of the world if you miss a match or tournament.
4. Recover the natural way. Rest the injured area and allow your recuperative powers to operate. If there is bleeding and swelling, ice treatment may be beneficial. Ice should be applied at least four times during the first forty-eight-hour period—each application

lasting some ten minutes (wrap the ice in a wet towel).
5. Start using the damaged tissues slowly against small resistances once you have rested the injury. Rest is extremely important. Use high repetitions to strengthen the area. Swimming is a tremendous exercise while you are recovering and can help enormously in your recuperation. Do *not* rush back into strenuous activity.
6. Once the injury has healed, do exercises to strengthen that area to prevent a recurrence of the injury.
7. Improve your flexibility (see Chapter 15).

To reiterate, these observations I have formed from my own personal experience. You may find them useful if you are in the invidious position of suffering from tennis elbow and considering a cortisone shot. The questions I would like you to ask yourself and your doctor are, for example: 'What does the physiotherapist say?' 'If I change my grip, will that improve matters?' 'Can I not afford to rest from squash for a month, continue running and start swimming?'

WARM-DOWN

The rationale for warming-down is persuasively presented in Watts, Wilson and Horwill, *op. cit.* p. 62:

The practice of going for a gentle jog after racing and training cannot be too highly recommended. When exercise ceases, the blood flow back to the heart is no longer assisted by the pumping action of the muscles;

[1] Causes and treatment of many injuries are discussed in D. Watts, H. Wilson and F. Horwill, *The Complete Middle Distance Runner*, Stanley Paul, 1974, pp. 105–20. The interested reader may also wish to consult G. Sheehan, *Encyclopedia of Athletic Medicine*, Runner's World Magazine, California, 1972.

[2] My view is reinforced to a degree by Dr G. Sheehan: 'Use of Butazolidine, steroid shots, and surgery have no place in the human engineering required in the treatment of overuse syndromes.' *Running and Being: The Total Experience*, Simon and Schuster, New York, 1978, p. 160.

this causes blood pooling and a build-up of pressure in the muscles which results in an accumulation of waste-product fluids. The result is stiffness the next day.

SUMMARY

* A warm-up routine enables the muscles to work with greater mechanical efficiency and reduces the likelihood of muscle injury.

* Prior to a match, exercises designed to stretch and warm the muscle groups in the body should be complemented by running and, if possible, hitting on a vacant court.

* When you have a match in the evening, it is a good idea, when possible, to play a couple of games in the morning.

* Warm-down after training or playing.

13. Training without the Ball

'The gods always favour the strong.' (Tacitus)

The task of writing about physical training proved almost as arduous as training itself! Merely for ease of exposition, I have split the discussion of training into training without and with a squash ball. The two chapters, however, must be viewed as a single entity.

I have tried to give a variety of types of training that can be done. It is essential that the reader choose from these a combination best suited to his aspirations and physical condition. This choice will, I hope, be made easier by the way in which the information is presented. In an attempt to avoid being bogged down in technicalities, I have written as simply as possible what I believe to be important.[1]

YOUNG PLAYERS

A common-sense warning to young players is appropriate here. Young people whose growth has not yet levelled off may be in danger of placing excessive strain on muscles already being stretched by rapid growth. It is particularly important that you play and enjoy your game, and that any training should be sub-maximal, that is at less than 100 per cent effort. After your training session, you should always feel that you could have done a little more.

TRAINING FOR WHAT?

A match can last anything from twenty minutes to two hours plus. The first game between Hunt and Zaman in the final of the British Open 1978 lasted fifty-one minutes! This fact makes a squash player's training schedule that much more involved than the average athlete's schedule, for the athlete knows the length of time that he is to exert himself.[2] On top of this, the movements performed in this time period vary enormously from back-pedalling towards the 'T' to tortuous twists. Thus training schedules have to equip the ambitious player with the physi-

[1] There are several excellent references to be consulted should you wish to become more familiar with the scientific foundation for training schedules. See, for example, D. K. Matthews and E. L. Fox, The Physiological Basis of Physical Education and Athletics, W. B. Saunders Company, Philadelphia, 1976.

[2] This is not to say that much cannot be learnt from the athlete. It is recommended that you read books written by the great athletic coaches such as Lydiard, Cerutty and Watts (see, for example, J. B. Gardner and J. Gerry Purdy, Computerized Running Training Programs, Tafners Press, California, 1975). In most of them you will find detailed schedules for all levels of performance.

cal abilities to twist and turn, dart and retreat, at varying intensities, for long periods of time. Moreover, the training must equip the player with the necessary racket skills, agility and co-ordination to subdue an aggressive opponent and, hopefully, force his submission.

FITNESS IS SPECIFIC

A cardinal aspect of fitness is its specificity. That is, an athlete trained to run 800 metres will struggle to complete a standard marathon. He would struggle even more, and be stiff the following day, if he were to play squash. You train yourself to become fit for a specific activity. From this, it follows that the best form of training for squash is actually *playing squash*, preferably with an opponent who usually beats you.

ONE MAN'S MEAT

Training schedules need to take account of the individual's physique and personality. In the general discussion that follows, you ought to experiment with the ideas presented, but tailor your schedule to your ambitions (we each have our own Everest), the time available to train and to your own particular mental and physical make-up.

It is for this reason that no one schedule has been presented. Geoff Hunt's weekly routine prior to the 1978 British circuit is given below to show how the then number one in the squash world prepared for a circuit. It is useful to study the types and combinations of training he utilized, the inten-

sity of his work effort, the repetitions and the intervals.

CONSISTENCY

An essential ingredient to realizing ambitions is consistency in training. It is of little use to train (or strain) like a demon for one week and then razzle wildly for the next. That sort of routine, or lack of routine, will do more harm than good, as in trying to catch up continuously you may well run down your metabolism.

CONDITIONING RUNNING

A cardinal principle of training is to begin slowly and diligently. Depending upon your present physical condition there is much to be said for beginning a planned schedule with the Lydiard-type long-distance conditioning running.[3] Build up your mileage slowly and in this way dig solid foundations upon which you are able to improve your performances further through interval running and very high-intensity work.

FORMAL SCHEDULE WITH VARIETY

The great advantage of a training schedule (preferably written out) is that it enables you to progress step by step, it ensures variety in your training and the attempt, at least, to get the correct combina-

[3] A. Lydiard and G. Gilmour, Run to the Top, Minerva Ltd, Auckland, 1967.

tion or mixture of the various types of training.

'Biting the bullet' every day can do positive physical harm besides dulling the enthusiasm for training. The greater the variety in the training, the more likely that the enthusiasm will be kindled and this is essential to bring out the required consistency and quality of effort. Training must be enjoyable, if only in retrospect from the sense of satisfaction of a job well done.

As mentioned earlier, fitness acquired from any training is specific. From this, we know that the best method of training is to play. But most of us would die of boredom spending hour upon hour every day on court. It is necessary to complement court routines and games with training in a gymnasium, on a track, in a park or on the road. Variety in training and in the environment in which you train keeps you mentally and physically more alert. Moreover, you acquire a better balanced physical development—squash alone builds up certain sets of muscles more than others.

TYPES OF TRAINING

There are, broadly speaking, three types of training: to increase stamina, muscle endurance and speed. The benefits from these forms of training do overlap, as speed training, for example, will improve stamina. Training can be done both on and off the court, with and without a ball. The problem is to get the balance which best suits you personally. Let us start from step one by considering what training geared to improved stamina, muscle endurance and speed involves.

STAMINA

Stamina is increased by long runs, or by playing long protracted rallies, routines or matches. Stamina-building may be likened to ensuring that a car's engine components are clean, well-oiled where necessary, and in good condition. Continuing this metaphor, it is of little use to fit twin carburettors to an engine which has faulty, ill-fitting parts which have not been correctly lubricated. Trying to race this car will lead to the engine seizing or collapsing. In like vein, the body must be conditioned through long-distance running before muscle endurance and speed work are attempted.

Stamina-building training is done ideally in the off-season. The squash player, who has kept himself reasonably fit and trim, should start running, preferably on soft surfaces, a few miles a day. Pulse rate can be maintained around 130–150 beats per minute. It is probably easiest to measure your pulse by placing your fingers at the base of your neck. To get an approximation for beats per minute, count your pulse for six seconds and add a nought to the number. You should also find that your resting pulse, taken first thing in the morning, decreases once you begin distance running. Build up the weekly mileage slowly but surely. Try to run between fifty and eighty km (thirty and fifty miles) a week. (If you wished to be a good athlete, 77

Mr Lydiard would want you to build up to 100 miles a week!) Time permitting, the player should continue playing two or three times a week—after the divorce, you will find you have more time!

Remember, build slowly:

Keeping close to the schedule means that the tempo of work is increased without creating great oxygen debts continuously, day after day, thereby lowering the runner's pH and upsetting his metabolism. (Lydiard and Gilmour, p. 56.)

MUSCLE ENDURANCE

Once you have been running the suggested distances for a couple of weeks, you can introduce intervals of fast running into the conditioning runs. The justification for this is that there is a greater training effect if you put more effort into your exercise. (The energy cost of muscle contraction increases more than proportionately with the increase in the speed of contraction. This explains why high-intensity work is so exhausting.)

The training schedule could read:

MONDAY Run five miles: include 4 × 300 m at a fast pace. The intervals run at a good pace can vary from around 200 to 600 m.

There should be a few days in the week when you run only the intervals. For example, Thursday's schedule may read:

THURSDAY Run 2×400 m, 2×300 m and 4×200 m all at $\frac{3}{4}$ pace.

This pace is still fast, i.e. pretty close to the limit (pulse rate around 180). There is a school of thought which maintains muscle endurance is best increased by running at the limit (flat-out) for sixty seconds. This, it is maintained, improves most effectively the ability to tolerate shortages of oxygen. The pulse rate should be forced above 180. The rest interval would be around five minutes (provided the pulse rate is below 120). If the pulse is still above 120, you have done enough repetitions. This type of workload, at very high intensity, is debilitating in the extreme—it really hurts! It should not be done on consecutive days, possibly only twice a week.

To reiterate, muscle endurance and speed work can only accomplish their goals if the background mileage has been done.

ON-COURT ENDURANCE TRAINING

Much endurance work can be done on court. It is important to practise the squash movement, particularly when the squash season draws near. There are many permutations of movement combinations, intensities, duration of effort, intervals of rest and repetitions. In selecting a particular work-load, the rule to be borne in mind is to increase slowly the quantity and quality of the effort.

Below is a brief description of some of the sequences of movements more commonly done on court. Generally players work on a 'one minute on, one minute off' basis. This is useful especially if you are working in pairs, as it enables the one to rest whilst the other performs. It is better to work with a friend as it is easier to suffer together.

1. Random running or ghosting

Run for one minute with racket in hand and simulate a tough rally in a squash match. That is, you will move to all areas of the court during the minute, hitting at an imaginary ball. Recover the 'T' after each shot. Because this work is purely physical, the player should twist and turn, stop and start frequently during the minute. The pulse should be kept around the 160-plus beats per minute so that it falls below 120 after the minute's interval. You are then ready for the next one minute's effort.

2. Pattern running or running stars

This form of on-court training is very similar to ghosting except that you run a particular pattern. It has the advantage that the runner is able to assess the quality of his effort by the number of movements completed. Random running, on the other hand, has the advantage of more closely approximating an actual rally.

A suggested pattern of movement would be running to each corner (see Fig. 74). Or you might consider including shots from the 'T' area—turning the star into a Star of David.

3. Running to numbers

When there are two players wanting to do court running it is often a good idea to number the areas on

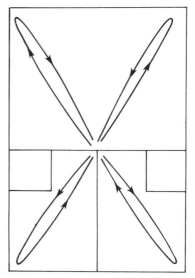

Fig. 74

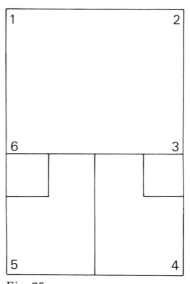

Fig. 75

court as in Fig. 75. The pattern of running is dictated by the resting or 'sleeping' partner as he shouts numbers which direct the active partner's movements. Then roles are reversed and revenge is often sweet!

4. Lengths

It is useful to run the length of the court—sets of twenty lengths are often done as this takes around sixty seconds. Running lengths is sensible when there are more than two players wishing to train. The pulse rate (again) provides a useful guide as to the required interval and the number of repetitions.

5. Across the court

Players may wish to practise movement across the court. Starting on the 'T' and running towards the 'forehand' side wall, you would lead with your right foot. This enables you to hit the forehand with the left leg leading. The steps are best explained using diagrams (see Figs. 76–78).

> Step 1: place right foot on the edge of the box
> Step 2: play forehand
> Step 3: kick off on the left leg and swivel towards the 'T' so that the left foot is on the edge of the box
> Step 4: right foot on to the 'T'
> Step 5: left foot on to the box
> Step 6: playing the backhand in the classical position with the right leg leading
> Steps 7 and 8: return to starting position.

This sounds complicated, but it is in fact very easy. All you are practising is efficient movement to the side walls so that you play shots in the classical position.

SPEED

Training to improve speed is done at the limit for a relatively short time period—anywhere between

Fig. 76

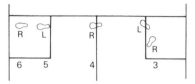

Fig. 77

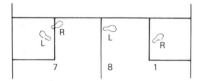

Fig. 78

five to thirty seconds. The rest period is such that the next repetition may be done flat-out. An athlete may do, for example, 8 × 50 m sprinting, each effort interspersed with slow jogging until the pulse has slowed down to below 120 bpm. He might then repeat this schedule after a five-minute rest. Hockey players run shuttles: on the training field will be marked out 5 m distances up to 25 m; the hockey players will race from the starting line to the 5 m mark, whirl around back to the starting line, whirl around to the 10 m mark and back to the start, to the 15 m mark and back and so on—a total of 150 m. They look to six sets of shuttles around thirty seconds each with a one-minute interval.

A squash player should borrow some of these ideas, but will also do sessions in which he will repeat specific squash movements.

THE COMBINATION

Choosing the combination of the types of training and specifying the actual schedule is no easy task. It will depend, to a degree, upon when next the player wishes to reach peak fitness and, of course, on ambitions. Ideally the player should hit a physical pinnacle (having honed a well-conditioned body with high intensity work both on and off court), relax for about ten days and then resume the building process with conditioning running. Unfortunately a squash player often wishes to play well in league each week and compete to the best of his ability in various tournaments. It is mainly during the off-season that he has to fit in his off-court training. During the season he has to stay close to a court to be able to improve ball control and to maintain, at least, his squash fitness. Yet, during the season it is often most beneficial physically and mentally to have a long run a week and, if possible, to fit in some interval training and speed work away from the court.

Another factor affecting a squash player's pattern of training is the time horizon of his goals. Is he only interested in performances in the immediate future, or is he interested in becoming a top player irrespective of the sacrifices to be made? Hard work is rewarded, not necessarily in the particular season in which it is done, but eventually the benefits of conscientious training will manifest themselves.

To a certain extent the body itself must dictate the training. That is, there must be a little flexibility allowed in the schedule. If the body is stiff and sore, still depleted from the previous session's load (or accidental overload), it is pointless flogging it further trying to do a speed session. Probably a three-mile stride in the country would be of greater benefit to both mind and body.

HUNT'S SCHEDULE

Geoff Hunt left Australia to play the 1978 British circuit, in his own words, 'the fittest ever'. He had built up to doing 13×800 m and 30×400 m, obviously not on the same day—nevertheless, incredible outputs. Geoff's weekly running programme was approximately as follows:

DAY 1: 400 m in 75 sec with 45 sec recovery—he built up to completing over 30 repetitions.
DAY 2: Long run of 8 miles.
DAY 3: 800 m in 2.35 min with 1.25 min recovery which he built up to 13 repetitions.
DAY 4: Rest day from running.

Geoff ran 400m and 800m at a pace which avoids excessive accumulation of lactic acid (that heavy-legged feeling). In this way he was able to do a greater number of repetitions.

On top of this, Geoff was still playing squash each day. In Melbourne there was no serious opposition for him to compete against, but his playing shows his belief in remaining closely in touch with the game between circuits. Geoff would also try to fit in some speed work in the form of 100m sprints and do exercises and light weights at home.

Despite this awesome schedule, **81**

Geoff lost in the first two tournaments of the British circuit. But with diligent practice on court twice a day after arriving in England, he won the third tournament at Chichester beating Mohibullah Khan in four.

Geoff Hunt's struggle proves that there is no substitute for match practice to sharpen one's game and physique. Jonah Barrington learnt the same lesson when he was still top dog in the world.

After I had written this chapter, I was able to watch with much interest the final of the 1978 British Open: Hunt versus Zaman. What a match! Jonah Barrington afterwards described the first game of fifty-one minutes' duration as the cruellest ever first game he had seen. Hunt's superb physical condition triumphed over Zaman's wizardry. The score in the first game was still 2-all after twenty minutes of long and incredibly gruelling rallies with Hunt doing some breathtaking retrieving. Yet when Zaman did win the first game 9–7, having played some brilliant squash, he was only able to offer relatively token opposition in the remaining three games. Hunt won them 9–1, 9–1, 9–2.

Rex Bellamy of The Times described the match thus (The Times, 10 April 1978, p. 8):

This was one of Hunt's finest performances. During the 50-minute first game, probably the longest (and one of the best) in the history of the championship, he endured a physical stress that would have devastated the resources of almost any other player. Zaman's stroke-play was superb. Hunt incurred a cruelly heavy cost in energy as he hurtled to and fro and bent and stretched in a mostly successful attempt to resist his tormentor. Under this terrible pressure the precision of Hunt's returns was astonishing. But Zaman hit 13 winners, won the game—and was four years the younger man.

Logically, that draining and ultimately disconcerting game should have been the end of Hunt. But this marvellous athlete managed to increase the pressure by taking the ball earlier—a formidably strenuous exercise—and going for more shots. Zaman slowed down, fading both physically and mentally because the first game had taken so much out of him. He began to look for easy points: and that, inevitably, meant easy points for Hunt. The Australian kept the accelerator 'flat on the boards' and never gave Zaman time for a breather.

In spite of the speed with which he played them, Hunt's shots were perfectly tailored to the task of repeatedly changing the pace and shifting Zaman from corner to corner at what would have been top speed had Zaman still been capable of it. Hunt was even finding the nick with his angles and boasts.

It was unreasonable that, after the first game, he should thus increase both the tempo and quality of his squash. But he did.

WEIGHT TRAINING

'Even the bravest cannot fight beyond his strength.' (Homer)

Weight training with high repetitions is a fruitful way of conditioning and strengthening the body.[4] It is sufficiently different from other forms of training to ensure that the enthusiasm for training is kept at a high level. Weight training can lead to a more balanced development of the body—this can reduce the risk of injury—and it can benefit the cardio-vascular system if done with high repetitions and each exercise completed in quick succession. Moreover, power translates to speed.

A schedule might include squats, with light dumb-bells, for one minute—that is, as many squats as possible to be done in a minute. This might be followed by burpees, bench climbing, sit-ups, bench presses, arm curls, chin-ups, lunges and the like, all in quick succession. This type of schedule is guaranteed to raise a sweat (and the pulse!).

John Short, probably the best-known coach of South African athletes, runs a most successful gymnasium in Pretoria. Each day he places on a notice board a programme which he calls the 'Surprise'. He encourages the gym's members to do the 'Surprise' as it is refreshing not to have to repeat a programme day after day. The 'Surprise' will always include some running on the spot and usually hits a particular muscle group, for example the shoulders, a little more severely than the rest of the body. Sometimes the programme hits all the muscles—or so it feels! The following day the 'Surprise' might contain a lot of stomach and leg work, and tax the cardio-vascular system.

John also has programmes which he has designed specifically for certain sports. Overleaf is one of his squash work-outs. You will notice that there is only a thirty-second rest after each set—this is designed to keep the pulse high (preferably above 150 beats per minute). In fact, the accent for the squash programmes is very much upon cardio-vascular development and improving muscle endurance. You first attempt the programme working through the sets and repetitions as scheduled in column 1. As you become accustomed to this schedule you will work through the progressively harder schedules. That is, you start slowly and build up the severity of the programme as you grow used to its load. (This principle of progressive loading should underlie all types of training schedules.) Once you have worked up to column 3, you can start increasing the weights used. Complete each exercise before continuing with the next exercise. For example, in the table overleaf in column 1 below you would do three sets of arm curls before starting the bench climbing.

An explanatory note on the exercises may be useful. 'Sponge running $3\frac{15}{15}$' means running on the spot flat out (high knee raises) for 15 seconds and then jogging

[4] Interested readers should consult *Exercises for Runners*, World Publications, California, 1977, which contains much sensible information about working with weights. The topic 'weights for women' is covered on pp. 75–7.

Rest 30 seconds after each set	1	2	3
Sponge running	$3\frac{15}{15}$	$4\frac{30}{30}$	$5\frac{30}{30}$
Stand up and lie down (15% of body weight)	10	15	20
Alternate arm curl	3×30	4×30	5×30
Bench climbing	3×20	4×20	5×20
Sit ups	3×20	4×20	5×20
Lie on stomach—trunk raise 6 sec	15	18	20
On hands—alternate leg in and out	3×30	4×30	5×30
Forward bend arm pumping	3×30	4×30	5×30

S–T–R–E–T–C–H

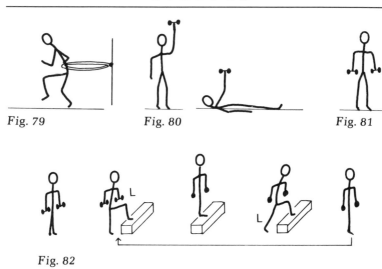

Fig. 79

Fig. 80

Fig. 81

Fig. 82

Fig. 83

Fig. 84

Fig. 85

for 15 seconds (total 3 mins). John has a rather ingenious way of simulating running (see Fig. 79). A bicycle tube is attached to the wall. The athlete puts the tube around his waist and runs against this resistance on a soft sponge surface.

'Stand up and lie down' is an exercise done with one dumb-bell held above the head. The arm supporting the weight is kept straight throughout the exercise (see Fig. 80). From the standing position you lower yourself until you lie flat on your back. From this position you struggle back to the standing position (you may use your free hand to aid getting up and down). Once the repetitions have been completed, you then repeat the exercise with the dumb-bell in the other hand.

'Alternate arm curls' is primarily an exercise for the biceps (see Fig. 81). With a dumb-bell in each hand, you raise the weight to shoulder level bending at the elbow. The upper part of the arm remains stationary. The exercise is done alternately right arm and then left arm, so that you raise only one weight at a time.

'Bench climbing' is usually done with dumb-bells in each hand. It is an excellent leg exercise. The 'bench' is to be approximately 45 cm (18 in) high. Starting with the left leg, you climb on to the bench and then down again (see Fig. 82). Do the required repetitions and then repeat with the right leg leading. This then will be one set completed.

'Sit ups' require no explanation. Lying on the stomach raising the trunk is also largely self-explanatory, although Fig. 83 may be helpful.

'On hands—alternate leg in and out' requires the normal press-up starting position. Each leg is then shot forward and backward alternately (see Fig. 84). The foot is to come as far forward as possible. To count repetitions, count only when the right leg comes forward.

'Forward bend arm pumping' is done with dumb-bells in each hand (see Fig. 85). The weights are then alternately raised and lowered as fast as possible to the chest.

OTHER SPORTS

A keen, conscientious sportsman with a preference for one sport, will almost definitely benefit from participation in other sports, as skills are often complementary. A little tennis practice for the squash player is likely to improve his volleying ability. Hiddy Jahan played much badminton as a junior and this may explain his wonderfully deceptive wrist action on the squash court.

SWIMMING

Swimming is an excellent supplement to the hard training a squash player should do. Unless the player does flexibility exercises (see Chapter 15), he will find himself with shortened muscle groups—in particular the back of the leg—and swimming is an exercise which seems to improve an athlete's suppleness. It can also be a gentle and rhythmic form of exercise and can be used therapeutically by a squash player after a hard physical work-out. On top of this, swimming forces regular breathing and can do much to expand lung capacity.

Swimming is also great when a player is plagued by an injury. This is particularly the case when it is a back injury—but do consult a specialist first. Training in water can be extremely useful when there is an injury below knee level, for example, a bruised heel or a strained achilles tendon. Training can be done in water, where one is unable to stand, by running in the water (to stay afloat). This is very severe on the quadriceps and is excellent for the heart and lungs. One could work on the 'one minute on, one minute off' basis.

SUMMARY

* Fitness is specific.
* Tailor the schedule to suit your physiology, ambitions and the time available to train.
* Start from a humble schedule and progressively increase the work rate. 'Train don't strain!'
* Train consistently with plenty of refreshing variation in the schedules.
* Build up. stamina through steady mileage before attempting to hone up your speed and increase your tolerance to lack of oxygen.
* To improve muscle endurance push up the pulse rate to 160 plus (preferably over 180) for up to one minute. Let the pulse rate determine the rest period and the number of repetitions. This type of work should improve the ability to supply energy for a longer period from a source which does not require oxygen and it should help the body cope with the accumulation of lactic acid in the muscles.
* Training to increase speed should be done at the limit. Emphasis is to be on the quality of the performance.
* Both muscle endurance and speed training should be done both on and off court.
* Weight training can lead to a more balanced development of the body and is useful as a variation in training routines.
* Skills acquired in other sports are often complementary to those required in squash.
* Swimming can aid recovery from certain injuries and is a good complement to a squash-training schedule.

14. Training with the Ball

Perfect practice makes perfect.

DUAL ROUTINES

It is envisaged that from the many routines described you will choose a series in which, most importantly, you practise shots you wish to develop and those which you hit badly. On top of this, you should construct a sequence of routines which will tax you physically. It is suggested that you arrange a training session so that a relatively static routine follows one which involves a great deal of movement. In this way the work-load can be extended as great oxygen debts are avoided and the ability to co-ordinate lasts that much longer.

The emphasis in a dual routine is placed upon getting the drill working. For example, if your partner is to drive to length off your drop shot, you should not be trying to hit the nick on your drop. Rather, deliberately play the ball 15 cm (6 in) away from the side wall and a little higher on the front wall than in match conditions. You still benefit as you learn to control the ball in the front of the court. Because the drill runs smoothly you are able to practise that many more shots in a given time period. On top of this, without unnecessary stoppages, the training effect is greater.

During a drill ensure that you practise good movement and watch your partner as if you did not know what his next shot would be. In fact, cultivate good habits—but remember to practise as much as a quarter of the shots off the 'wrong' foot. In the routines where both you and your partner have a choice of shots and thereby introduce an element of uncertainty into the routine, the more closely the drill approximates a rally in a match.

The fifteen basic drills given below do not exhaust all the possible combinations of shots. You are encouraged to invent and modify routines to suit you better. The routines have been divided into static routines, where little movement is involved: dynamic routines, where both players cover much ground; and static/dynamic routines, where one player is basically feeding the other. All these practices are to be done at least twice—the partners swopping roles. The routines which involve four repetitions will be specifically mentioned. The time spent on each routine should be built up to about three minutes. If there are four changes to complete a routine, it will take about twelve minutes. Given a normal time constraint, it is essential that you choose from these fifteen routines a series which best suit your own and your friend's requirements.

The letters A and B represent two players. Unless specified to the contrary, the terms, drive, lob, drop or smash, imply down-the-wall shots.

STATIC ROUTINES

1. A cross-court drives, B boasts

A drives the ball, from the front of the court, deep and wide across the court. B boasts the ball back to A. A drives cross-court and so on (see Fig. 86). This routine will be done four times with each player spending time in each corner. B should practise the various types of boast and A practises hitting across the court out of reach of an imaginary opponent on the 'T'. His cross-court should be struck high and hard to hit the side wall, without a bounce, somewhere in the service-box area.

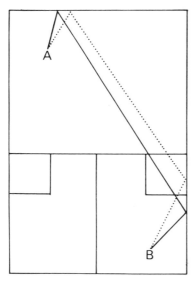

Fig. 86

2. A lobs cross court, B smashes to length then boasts, A lobs ...

This routine will be done four times with each player smashing to length on both backhand and forehand sides of the court (see Fig. 87).

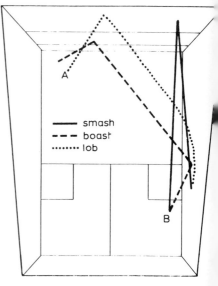

Fig. 87

DYNAMIC ROUTINES

1. A boasts from deep in the court, B drops, A lobs across the court, B smashes to length, A boasts ...

This is explained most easily in a diagram (see Fig. 88). This routine is to be repeated four times with each player boasting on both sides of the court.

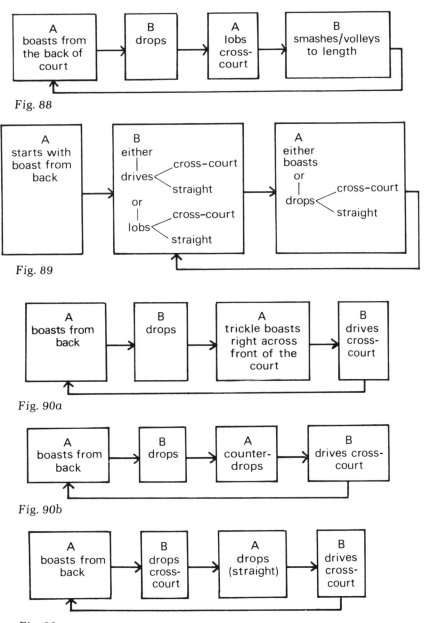

Fig. 88

Fig. 89

Fig. 90a

Fig. 90b

Fig. 90c

2. A boasts from deep in the court, B drops, A drives to length, B boasts, A drops ...

This sequence repeats itself: boast, drop, drive; boast, drop, drive, and so on. The routine is to be done twice. Each player must have a turn at boasting on the forehand and on the backhand.

3. Boast and drive

The simplest boast and drive schedule is where A boasts from the back of the court and B drives to length. Both A and B should recover the 'T' after striking the ball. To ensure that both players remain alert, the man in front can be given the option to hit occasionally a cross-court drive. Similarly the man behind should occasionally be allowed to hit a drop instead of a boast.

4. Lob and volley boast

This routine is similar to the boast and drive routine except that A will lob the ball down the wall and B will hit the volley boast.

5. Drive or lob, boast or drop

Start with the boast from the back of the court. Again, it is easier to illustrate this routine diagrammatically (see Fig. 89).

6. The big variation

The different sequences of this routine are shown in Fig. 90. The middle sequence is to be repeated four times.

STATIC/DYNAMIC ROUTINES

1. Volley exercise

A is to move along the 'T' parallel to the front wall volleying everything *down the wall* to length. B feeds A from the back of the court and can hit the ball either down the wall *or* across the court. B's task is to allow A to develop a rhythm yet to stretch and twist him. Usually A sets out to practise volleying only to length but A might be given the choice of practising straight short kills if B feeds him an easy opening.

2. A hits anywhere, B boasts

A positions himself in the front centre of the court and starts the routine. A can hit the ball anywhere on the court and B must boast the ball so that it returns to A. A's objective is to make B do plenty of work and B must try to avoid errors. This is a very severe routine—the Pakistani players use it, particularly when their coach gets hold of them!

3. Short stress or murders

The name 'murders' is appropriate (as you will realize once you have attempted this routine). A stands in the service box and moves *very little* as B must hit the ball *to* him. A can hit the ball anywhere in the front of the court, B, of course, never allows the ball to bounce twice and returns the ball *nicely* to A. This routine is done four times as each player feeds from each service box. I would suggest starting out doing intervals of thirty–forty-five seconds. Remember that the ball must be played so that the player feeding is always on balance—the unfortunate (running) partner is *not* practising length.

4. Drop-shot practice

A, remaining in the front of the court, feeds the ball down the wall to B who practises his straight drop shot. A can feed the ball so that B practises his drop from the front, middle and back on one side of the court. B should also be fed balls that he can volley short. A and B then switch roles, and then work down the other side of the court. Exactly the same format is observed when practising the cross-court drop into the nick (or volley drop).

5. Lob exercise

A, who has the role of feeding the ball, remains in the back of the court. B starts off from the 'T' and should recover the 'T' after each lob. A can hit the ball anywhere in the front of the court and as he strikes the ball must shout either 'cross' or 'straight'. If A instructs 'cross', B must lob the ball across the court. If 'straight' is shouted, B floats the ball high down the side wall. A should hit straight and cross-court drops and the different types of angles (including the reverse angle).

6. Hitting hard to length

A remains in the back of the court and feeds the ball down the wall, so that B can hit it in front of the 'T' (either on the volley or once it has bounced). B hits the ball as hard as he can to length. The routine is to be done four times.

To make the exercise more interesting, you can keep score. If the ball bounces over the 'T' *and* does not touch the side wall, the striker scores one point. If either it touches the side wall or bounces before the 'T', deduct one point from the score. You will find it difficult at first to build up a positive score.

7. A boasts or drives and B drives across the court or floats down the wall

A has a relatively static position in the back of the court. He can either hit the ball down the wall or boast the ball. If he boasts the ball, B (positioned on the 'T') must reply with a wide cross-court drive. If A hits the ball down the wall, B tries to volley it back to length. If B is unable to volley the ball, he must move as economically as possible and play the ball from the back of the court to length (see Fig. 91).

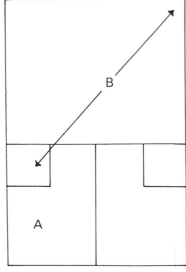

Fig. 91

This routine is repeated four times. Note that when A does decide to drive the ball, he should hit the ball in such a way as to encourage B to take it around the 'T' level. That is, A should hit a slow ball which probably would be short of a good length.

SINGLE ROUTINES

No guidelines have been suggested regarding the time to be spent on each routine. To a certain extent this will be determined by fatigue in the arm and, to a degree, by boredom. Obviously the more time spent practising shots the better. Like all efforts, however, rewards are subject to the law of diminishing returns. There is no substitute for diligent practice alone on court and it is recommended that you develop a set of routines (invent a few as well) which will improve and broaden your range of shots—even if you only do them three to four times a month. Try always to pay careful attention to detail. If you cannot complete a quality session, rather leave the practice until another day.

Single routines have the weakness that there is little uncertainty—you know where you will play the next shot. To compensate for this and to ensure some movement, it is suggested that when, for example, you feed yourself to practise forehands, you do the feeding on the backhand side. This will ensure that you move your feet. Remember to practise hitting some forehands and backhands off the 'wrong' foot.

1. Basic ball control

Start 1·5 m (5 ft) from the front wall (away from the side wall) and hit forehands, so that the ball just bounces in front of you. Do this until you can hit ten consecutive shots. Repeat the exercise, this time volleying each time. Then try the backhand. These are the four parts of the exercise. The objective is to improve your ball control—try to be able to hit each ball from the same position.

Once you have mastered ten consecutive shots, volleying and allowing the ball to bounce, move a further 1·5 m (5 ft) from the front wall and repeat the exercise. Once this has been successfully accomplished, move back another 1·5 m (5 ft). Continue practising this routine until you can control the ball expertly from the back of the court. This routine is not as easy as it may sound—try it!

2. Chipping

Practise volleying the ball around shoulder-height down the side wall on either wing. That is, stand in the service box and volley the ball high on to the front wall so that it returns to you at about shoulder height. Strive to volley the ball so that it runs parallel and as close as possible to the side wall.

3. Length

Hit the ball up and down the side wall hard to length. Try to hit the ball so that you play the next shot as the ball bounces off the back wall. That is, overhit the ball slightly each time.

Another useful way of practising length is to hit the ball so that it bounces, each time, in the back area of the service box. Vary the height and pace of each shot.

4. 'Reverse angles'

This routine is played from the 'T'. The ball is volleyed front wall/side wall so that it returns to the striker and he is able to volley the ball to the opposite side of the front wall. The sequence, as illustrated in Fig. 92, is repeated.

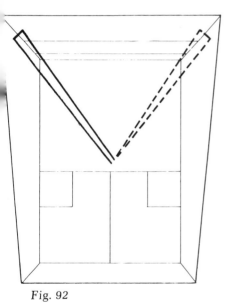

Fig. 92

This exercise helps develop a good wrist action and forces you to volley in front of the body. Note that a reverse angle is hit. That is, for a right-hander, the forehand volley is illustrated by the solid line. The exercise can be varied by allowing the ball to bounce before striking it. This variation makes the routine considerably easier.

5. Forehand drive, backhand drive

Stand in front of the 'T'. The ball is played on the forehand to hit side wall/front wall in the forehand court, returning to the player so that he may hit a backhand. The backhand shot is played to front wall/side wall (in the forehand court) so that the player is able to hit a forehand drive (see Fig. 93). The ball is struck each time so that it bounces before the player strikes it again. The routine is repeated in the other front corner.

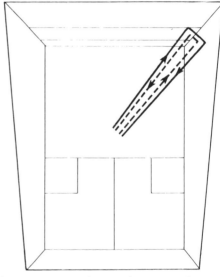

Forehand stroke (for the right-hander) – – –
Backhand stroke ———

Fig. 93

6. Taleb's drive practice

It is by no means certain that Taleb invented this method for practising drives, but he was the player I first saw using it. The player positions himself just in front of **93** the 'T' and then hits forehand drives, one after the other, to hit front wall/side wall. The drill is repeated on the backhand. (See Fig. 94.)

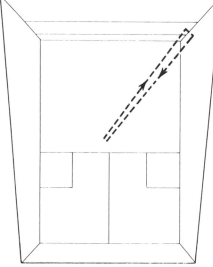

Fig. 94. *Taleb's drive practice*

7. Drop shots

If you wish to practise the forehand drop, set the shot up by hitting a *backhand* from the 'T' to hit front wall/side wall. Turn and be ready to hit the forehand drop. Similarly, to practise the backhand drop, set the ball up from a forehand stroke.

To practise the cross-court drop set yourself up in the same way, and try to keep the preparation for the shot the same as when hitting the straight drop. All these drop shots can and should be practised from all over the court.

8. The lob

An excellent way of practising the lob technique efficiently without letting the ball cool down is to practise lobbing parallel to the *front* wall. Treat each side wall as the front wall. Start out a little way in front of the 'T' facing the front wall. Hit a backhand lob high onto the right-hand side wall. The ball should rebound across the court, parallel to the front wall, high onto the left-hand side wall. Execute now a forehand lob onto the left-hand side wall. Remember to get height on your shot so that the ball rebounds high across the court. Backhand lobs alternate with forehand lobs.

9. The cross-court lob

To practise the backhand cross-court lob from the front of the court, hit a forehand boast from the 'T' and then toss the ball into the opposite back corner. Exactly the same applies for the forehand lob, except that you will set yourself up from a backhand boast. The exercise must be done snappily—quick movement is required to retrieve the ball and the boast must be firmly struck—otherwise the ball will get too cold.

There is a simple test to evaluate the quality of the cross-court lob. On the court chalk a line one racket's length away from the back wall in the corner to which you are *not* lobbing. If the ball rolls across the floor and touches the side wall between the back wall and the chalk mark, the lob was beautifully executed. If not, keep practising!

10. Overheads

An excellent method for practising overhead kills is to start as in the reverse angle routine (4) described above and within that drill to practise forehand and backhand kills (both straight and cross-court). That is, hit 'reverse angles' and then hit the volley kill—if possible, continue the routine without stopping, otherwise merely restart the routine.

Another way to practise the overhead is by lobbing to yourself and then hitting the overhead. Again it is best when practising the forehand overhead, for example, to hit a backhand lob. In this fashion you are able to experiment with, and indeed practise, swinging at the ball from the inside out and from the outside in (of the ball's arc).

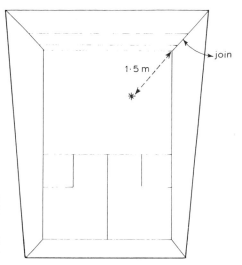

Fig. 95

Because you are uncertain of the angle at which the ball will return to you, this exercise should help tone up your reflexes and improve your ability to stop volley.

11. Boast into forecourt, then practise range of strokes

Set yourself up in the front of the court by boasting from the 'T'. Practise hitting (one after another) a complete range of shots: length, short kills, cross-courts (length and those designed to die short). You can also practise deceptive ploys, such as, for example, body movement in the direction opposite to that in which the ball is struck.

12. Hitting into the join

Stand approximately 1·5 m (5 ft) away from where the front wall meets the side wall (see Fig. 95). Repeatedly volley the ball for this join at about cut-line level.

13. The serve

Practising the serve is worthwhile. To keep the ball warm intersperse the slow serves with hard serves. Remember to vary the angle off the side wall and the pace of the serve.

CONDITIONED GAMES

It is often a good idea to practise certain aspects of your game during a practice match. The two most common games are the long game and the short game. In the long game both players are only allowed to hit to length. That is, if one player strikes a ball so that it bounces in front of the 'T', he immediately loses the point. In **95** the short game, the players may only hit so that the ball bounces short of the 'T'.

Conditioned games can also serve to reduce the difference in standard between the two competing players if the better player is limited to doing certain things. For example, the better player may only play in the front of the court or he may only hit the ball above the cut-line on the front wall.

Mike Symonds, one of South Africa's most thoughtful players/ coaches, recently demonstrated a conditioned game whereby each player may only hit a drive to length or a boast from the back of the court, and a cross-court lob or a drop from the front of the court. This game focuses the player's attention on the need for similar preparation for the drive and the boast, and for the lob and drop, to introduce an element of uncertainty into the opponent's mind. It will also force practice from each corner of the court—very often practice-partners both favour the backhand and, as a result, the practice-game may well be played predominantly in the left-half of the court.

TWO VERSUS ONE

When there are three players and only one court is available, it is often most pleasant and profitable to play two against one. The players take it in turn being 'two against one'. The 'two' usually play one on either side of the court. The object of the game is to move the single player as far and as fast as possible. The single player is out to survive the attack for as long as possible. To get maximum benefit from the game, mistakes must be minimized. A couple of useful hints: the unfortunate 'one' will find the lob a most effective shot; neither of the 'two' should frequently use the cross-court drive as his partner will usually be in the way. *Be careful of dangerous play.*

SUMMARY

* Select routines which will develop and strengthen your games.
* Order the sequence of dual routines so that the physically taxing ones are followed by less severe movements.
* In a dual routine the emphasis is placed upon getting the drill working.
* When feeding yourself in a single routine, ensure that there is some snappy movement between shots.
* Conditioned games, where shot patterns are limited, are a useful supplement to other forms of training. The types most commonly used are the long game and the short game. Conditioned games can effectively reduce the discrepancy in standards between two players.
* Two versus one games are excellent practice for improving your lobs and drops. They are also a pleasant way of increasing specific fitness.

15. Flexibility

Exercises to increase the body's flexibility or suppleness are most often neglected by squash players. Some players are ignorant as to the accumulating evidence on the importance of flexibility while others merely believe these exercises to be irrelevant.

We have touched upon the spin-off effect of improved flexibility on speed (Chapter 9: Movement) and the fact that stretching after arduous exercise may aid recovery, but, most importantly, stretching exercises are designed to prevent or minimize the risk of injury. Sports physiotherapist Joseph Zohar argues that muscles must be stretched to levels *above* the normal requirements of the sport as *abnormal* pulls and strains produce injuries. Obviously this can only be done outside the sport and Zohar suggests that yoga-type stretching appears best suited to meet this bill. The ambitious squash player especially must heed this advice as, with increased training and playing, various muscle groups tend to shorten.

DON'T BOB OR FORCE

In the exercises illustrated below, the positions must be held, without strain, for at least twenty seconds. Do not bob up and down as this invokes a reaction (the stretch reflex) which prevents the goal of increased flexibility from being achieved. Furthermore, do not force the body into painful positions, rather make moderate but regular demands upon it. The improvement in flexibility comes gradually—it is unrealistic to expect an immediate improvement given the fact that your present condition is the end result (probably) of many years of hard work which has strengthened and shortened certain muscle groups.

POSITIONS/ASANAS

The sequence of positions given below (Figs 96–105) are relatively simple. Ladies, in particular, may find them very easy. Once you have mastered these asanas or positions, it is recommended that you develop your own set of exercises from the more advanced

Fig. 96

Fig. 97

Fig. 100

Fig. 98

Fig. 101

Fig. 99

Fig. 102

Fig. 103

Fig. 104

Fig. 105

positions.[1] Most of the exercises below are taken from ones John Short encourages his athletes to do.

SUMMARY

* Stretching exercises are vital to minimize the risk of injury.

* Stretching must be done regularly and positions must be held, without strain, for about twenty seconds.

* Once the simple positions have been conquered, more advanced positions should be attempted.

[1] An excellent booklet, which does contain more advanced asanas, is *Exercises for Runners*, World Publications, California, 1977. It also provides a more detailed rationale for stretching, and references to Yoga books which could be of further use. Any interested reader is also referred to T. M. Travis, 'A Comparative Study of Three Stretching Techniques', Southern Illinois University thesis published in *Completed Research in Health, Physical Education and Recreation*, volume 12, 1970.

I recently came across a marvellous book called *Light on Yoga* by B. K. S. Iyengar (Unwin Paperbacks, 1979). Perhaps most interesting and useful were suggested curative asanas for various diseases contained in Appendix II.

Part IV

Just Talking

16. Just Talking

CHANGE YOUR WEAKNESS INTO STRENGTH

A possible reaction to reading this book might well be: 'That's all very interesting and stimulating, but I have limited time to concentrate upon squash. Where on earth do I begin?' You should start out with an analysis of your own game: 'Where am I weakest? Is it the backhand, is it overhead, is it in the forehand front corner, or is it my physical condition?' *Whatever the area you decide is weakest, that is where you concentrate your efforts.* The process of self-analysis is continuous as you improve, and dictates the area (sometimes areas) to which you pay special attention. It is often a good idea to sound out your practice partners' views on your weakest areas. Possibly you could ask an experienced player to watch you and analyse your game. Most players would be flattered by the request.

ATTENTION TO DETAIL

The difference between winning and losing is often very small. Each rally is vital. It is just as in athletics where the man who came second is that fraction slower than the winner. Leads had been swopped throughout the race, but somehow the winner had that little extra—possibly he hurled himself at the finishing line to snatch victory. If this is indeed the case, the best way to ensure that *you* are the victorious one is to pay careful attention to detail. Below are suggestions that may just add that extra lustre to tip the see-saw in your favour.

PHYSICAL PREPARATION

Training for an event should cease some forty-eight hours before the body is tested in combat. The forty-eight-hour break enables the body to recover from training so that prior to the match you feel strong. On top of this build-up period, many endurance athletes control their diet very strictly prior to a race. Åstrand advocates the following diet to maximize the muscle-glycogen stores:[1]

1. One week before the competition, exhaust the muscles primarily involved in the event. This will deplete their glycogen stores. This is required for a subsequent increase in glycogen storage.
2. Over the next three days, your diet should include mostly protein and fat. Such will maintain low muscle glycogen.

[1] As given in D. K. Mathews and E. L. Fox, *The Physiological Basis of Physical Education and Athletics*, W. B. Saunders Company, Philadelphia, 1976, pp. 404–5.

3. Following the three days of primarily protein and fat consumption, add large amounts of carbohydrate to the diet. (This is in addition to the fat and protein.)

This diet is not recommended for activities of a short duration. The increased glycogen level is often accompanied by a feeling of stiffness and heaviness as the water content of the muscles increases with the glycogen build-up.

I have not known any squash player who claims improved physical performance as a result of this attempt to increase the muscle-glycogen level. Single squash matches are rare, but this diet might be useful when an unusual one-off affair is at stake. However, a squash tournament often places enormous *daily* strain on the body as the player advances in the tournament, and all serious squash players certainly do watch their food intake prior to a match. It is difficult (as always!) to generalize, but many players eat a small, predominantly carbohydrate, meal some six hours prior to a big match.[2] If thirsty, he could drink some tea with honey.[3]

As regards alcohol, the athlete has to be extremely wary. Certainly a beer, shandy or a pint of cider after a tough training session or match is unlikely to do any harm—in fact, it is probably good to drink a little as there is some nutritional value in beer, for example, and the alcohol will help relax you. The danger, of course, comes when the occasional beer becomes a daily beer and the daily beer two daily beers. The consumption of alcohol must be strictly controlled if an athlete is to realize his potential.

Smoking is a health hazard and cannot be condoned under *any* circumstances. There are a few good players who smoke but the risk to health, ignoring the effect on fitness, makes smoking a fool's past-time.

Turning from cigarettes to drugs, this chapter was written at the time of the 1978 World Cup in Argentina. The Scottish international footballer, Willie Johnston, had recently been sent home, his international career grinding to an ignominious end. He had admitted taking the drug Fencamfamin-hydrochloride, a stimulant, prior to the match against Peru. Whilst drugs, be they stimulants, steroids or cardio-respiratory aids, certainly will improve performance, there are a number of dangers attached to their use. Firstly, the longer term effects of these drugs have not been fully documented. Of more significance is the fact that some sportsmen have died as a result of taking drugs. But, to my mind, Christopher Brasher writing in the *Observer* (11 June 1978) provides a more persuasive denunciation of drugs in sport:

[2] Studies conclusively demonstrate that diets lacking in carbohydrates have deleterious effects on work performance. See Mathews and Fox, p. 404.

[3] While on the topic of nutrition, it is strongly recommended that the serious athlete consult *Food for Fitness* from World Publications (P.O. Box 366, Mt View, Calif. 94040, USA). This very readable series of articles brings to the sportsman the latest information on performance nutrition, and it is my view that this vital aspect of training has been sorely neglected.

Death is the final penalty but the life of a sportsman on drugs is a perpetual living penalty because he is offending against himself. A man's public image is as nothing compared to his own image of himself and if he knows that his success is based, in part, on drugs then his respect for himself is less than the respect awarded to him by others – and that amounts to living a lie.

Sleep often evades the tense sportsman, especially after a very tough match. It can be argued that the use of a sleeping tablet, *in these circumstances alone*, is beneficial. A non-barbiturate sedative, flurazepan hydrochloride (Dalmane), is often prescribed to sportsmen: it is thought not to be addictive and to be relatively safe, even if taken in quantity.

Jet lag, the effect on the body of flying aggravated by time changes, is a condition to be treated with care. Probably the most sensible thing to do after a long plane trip is to bath and go to bed. Forget about training and immediately getting used to the courts. Dr J. P. R. Williams, the brilliant Welsh full-back with an interest in sports-medicine, maintains that for each hour in the time change experienced, one extra day should be allocated to the period between arrival time and the first match. Thus when Wales left for Perth and experienced a seven-hour time change, they organized an itinerary which left them seven days to adjust to conditions before their first match. In squash, generally speaking, the longer the period to acclimatize to conditions the better. This is par-ticularly the case when conditions differ markedly—for example, when going from competing on cold courts in England to playing in hot, high-altitude conditions in South Africa. Thus Dr Williams's advice provides an absolute minimum period between time of arrival and competition.

MENTAL PREPARATION

You should be keyed-up for a match. Without a degree of tension it is impossible to play your best squash. Physiologically, as your body tenses up, additional supplies of adrenalin are pumped into the bloodstream causing a raised heart-beat and an increased level of blood sugar. Your strength and alertness increases and the body responds as if to a dangerous situation. Problems do arise when the tension is so great that it causes your muscles and tendons to harden and cramp your strokes.

The first step in controlling your nervous state is to recognize and accept this tension. The best mood in which to go on court is a feeling of quiet confidence: that you are going to win however well your opponent plays. This confidence comes in part with the knowledge that your physical preparation for the match has been adequate. At some stage in most close matches, one player mentally gives the game away and decides to drop his level of play 5 per cent down and accept a creditable loss. The great players have the ability to hold on just for a few seconds or minutes more than their opponents. Remember even winners have to surmount pain barriers; and a major requirement to break these barriers is the mental determination to do so.

The second step is to have a regular way of passing the time before a match. Perhaps reading the newspaper, listening to the radio, packing your kit, having a bath and then warming up. Do not forget to allow enough time to get to the courts before you are due to play. There is nothing worse than arriving five minutes late after an exhausting trip through traffic and finding your opponent sitting quietly in the changing-room. I prefer arriving already changed into squash clothes some fifteen minutes before the match.

Finally, have a game plan. Decide exactly how you are going to play your opponent. Avoid playing to his strengths—all players have a favourite stroke for winning a rally. And, equally important, decide what you are going to do if things go badly wrong. Hit high down the backhand/forehand wall? Lob? Increase the pace of your drives? Concentrate on length? Eliminate the backhand boast?

CLOTHING, SHOES AND RACKETS

Clothing should be clean and functional. You must look and feel smart. The functionality of clothing is important—it must not restrict movement. Moreover, the clothes should be loose-fitting and expose as large an area of skin surface as is deemed decent. This will aid heat loss, or heat dissipation, through evaporative cooling.

It is vital to have a comfortable pair of squash shoes that do not slip. New shoes should be worn-in during practice-matches before being donned for a match. The heel of the shoe should be comfortably padded to avoid bruising the foot.

As regards rackets, it is preferable to have at least two with which you know you are comfortable. Take a little trouble to ensure that the strings and grips are in a good state of repair.

THE KNOCK-UP

As has been mentioned, it is a good idea to hit up on a vacant court (not the court on which you will play the match) just prior to the match. The knock-up period is used to find a length on the court and to practise a wide range of strokes. Shots should be attempted when you are perfectly set up for them. The knock-up should be used to increase confidence, so do not hit five drops in the tin, make sure they go up. It is certainly not to be used to see who can hit the most nicks. It is disappointing to see the number of young players who always 'win' the knock-up, yet never seem to win the match.

Whilst on the follies of certain young players, it is perhaps worthwhile noting that there seem to be many who, without any track record to speak of, seem to know it all. A brash, arrogant youngster may not want to be helped by the older, more experienced players. Yet many of these players *are* worth listening to. A quietly confident junior keen to learn is more likely to find the odd 'godfather' who takes an interest in his progress and who may well be able to pinpoint weaknesses and suggest valuable short cuts.

BROKEN BALL

When the ball breaks during a match, it is essential that you get used to the new one before playing delicate shots. Often before a ball has settled down, it is difficult to control and an advantage might be gained by hitting the ball hard to length. Reluctant as one may be to change a winning pattern, a new ball must be treated with respect and temporarily one should allow the newness of the ball to dictate the pattern of play.

CRAMP

In high humidity, where the body's ability to cool itself is impaired, in high temperatures or when you have to play twice a day, you may have problems of cramping. If so, it is worthwhile experimenting with either slow sodium or slow potassium tablets. Before doing so, however, consult your doctor so that together you can design an experiment to determine what best suits your metabolism. Adequate fluid intake, preferably water, probably remains the best precaution taken against cramping.

FLUID INTAKE

For a long time it was generally accepted by squash players that one should not drink anything between games. Recent findings, however, have established that this view is erroneous. Fluids *should* be replaced. The actual make-up of the liquid is less important than the fact that you ought to drink fluids between games. In any event, there is no general agreement as to the optimal mix of ingredients, but the trend in opinion seems to be towards very weak salt and/or glucose solutions. The ideal temperature of the drink is thought to be 5°C.

Many players find a diluted 'isotonic' drink (for example, 'Game', 'Accolade', 'Staminade') most beneficial. There is, however, much to be said for drinking about half a glass of water between each game. Fruit juices after the match and well-balanced meals should soon restore the mineral and salt balance in the body.

COACHING EXPERIENCE

It is sometimes rather frustrating that, having told a group of youngsters exactly how Jahangir plays, they do not do so 'exactly' as he does! A pupil takes time to absorb all you have to teach him. It is often pointless to be demonstrating how the ball may be faded across the front of the court when he scarcely has the ability to hit the ball to length.

As South Africa's national coach for some three years, I was involved with many top coaches and had the pleasure of teaching talented and enthusiastic juniors. When interacting with them I never failed to learn something. When running a national squad week we would ask the day's guest coach, after he had spoken on some aspect of the game, what he regarded as the most significant thing he had learned in his career. That is, what was the changed perception or activity which had resulted in the most dramatic improvement in his game. These revelations always had a marked impact on the juniors, and based on some of these revelations I have compiled a list of ten pointers that I would like to have been *fully* aware of at an early stage of my career. In retrospect, I seemed such a terribly slow learner. The points made are by no means exhaustive and should be seen as complementary to Geoff Hunt's famous ten guide-lines. Some indeed merely repeat what Geoff has stated and what was written earlier in this book, but they may be useful as a check-list to be referred to periodically:

1. Length

Be sure to get your opponent playing shots *right in the back corners*. A good cross-court drive or lob which strikes the side wall does have the advantage that this impact slows down the ball so that it dies closer to the back wall. Ensure that the cross-court is wide of the opponent's volley-arc. It is useful to think of two types of length, namely, defensive and attacking. When you are defending you should strike the ball aiming for a first bounce in the nick at the back of the court. On attack, you may well prefer to hit the ball harder and lower so that it bounces for the second time in the back-court nick.

If the ball is struck to a good length, especially if it is tight to the side wall, then you *limit your opponent's options*. That is, he would be most unwise to attempt a cross-court nick shot.

Finally, never under-estimate the effectiveness of the lob.

2. Go forward

Volley the ball and prepare early for your shot, i.e., avoid a rushed backswing.

3. Working shots

When you attack the front of the court, do not hit a winner *or* a loser. Be confident that you will not make the error. Very often your next shot to length is the winner. Count your unforced errors per practice-game and ensure that the tally reduces.

4. Tactics

There are no rigid rules here as they must depend to a large degree on your opponent—his position, abilities (and the score). Two guidelines may be useful:
  (i) Hit the shot which enables you to recover the 'T' before the opponent strikes the ball.
  (ii) The opponent is potentially more dangerous in the front of the court.

5. Training

Train with the primary objective of *making your opponent work*. With this goal in mind, racket skills will not be neglected.

Remember that fitness is specific.

6. Strengths and superstrengths

Devote much of your training sessions to eliminating weaknesses, but do not forget to work on the *development* of your total game. Try, for example, to add a dimension to your game which is exceptional in the sense of your ability to execute it, i.e., 'never' miss a crosscourt nick or a three-wall boast. You may also try to introduce a new dimension. For example, learn to cut the ball short (both straight and across the court) using an open-faced racket to take the pace off the ball.

7. Focus attention on the ball during matches

Forget about what you are doing at the top of your backswing. Play the match according to your preplanned strategy confident in the good habits that you have acquired from conscientious training.

8. Determination

Certainly 'gutsiness' or the ability to 'hang-in' is partly a result of socialized behaviour, environmental and possibly genetic factors. But perhaps most important of all is a player's expectation of himself. This expectation can be enhanced by diligent and disciplined preparation. The greater one's preparation, the more likely one is to acquire a quiet, but enormously powerful, self-confidence. Self-imposed constraints to one's progress recede into the distance— you now *owe* it to yourself to compete to your maximum ability.

Each rally counts although only the last rally counts. To explain this seemingly paradoxical statement is simple. All the previous rallies combined will determine who wins the last rally.

9. Quality

There must always be an intense desire for *perfection*. Fractional improvements can make a big difference to your game.

10. Diary

Record your training activities. This will help you to establish the schedule most suited to you. It may also serve as a source of inspiration—after all you cannot have a blank page!

Two relatively minor points are also worth bearing in mind. If the ball is tight to the side wall, consider playing the shot with a stiff wrist and try to hit the ball high down the wall to length. Secondly, if the ball comes to you at an unexpected angle having struck the join between the front and side walls, ignore the temptation to play short and hit that shot to length.

PLAY TO WIN

'Winning isn't everything, it's the only thing.' (Vince Lombardi)

Winning is indeed not everything. Much satisfaction can and should be derived from playing 'well'. Yet, I believe, a player must always play to win. If you do not play to win, then you might as well not bother keeping the score.

The sensation of winning—the elation, the empathy and anticlimax—has been beautifully described by Jonah Barrington in an interview extracted from the *Sunday Times* magazine, London, 15th September 1974:

There is a fantastic and savage and unrivalled and unbelievable satisfaction at the moment when you know you have beaten your opponent. There is simply no feeling on Earth quite like it—it is a primitive thing, a conquest, a triumph, an utter victory. You look into his eyes and you see the defeat there, the degradation, the humiliation, the beaten look and there isn't anything in the world like it. . . . Mind you, the feeling only lasts for a split second. Then you feel such compassion for him. And always afterwards, the depression, the dreadful anticlimax.

Jonah's book, Murder in the Squash Court, is quite outstanding and is well worth reading.

AGE

It might well be appropriate to talk about age just after 'winning'. There will come a time when you will not win at a particular level—somebody will eventually beat Jahangir. But when should one stop playing squash? To my mind the obvious answer, ignoring the few people to whom squash is a livelihood, is to stop when you no longer enjoy competing or playing. A magical age of, say, forty-five or fifty should not dictate your retirement from the game. Fatalities are bound to occur on a squash court, or in bed or on the roads for that matter. Man is born to die and it is arguable that dying on a squash court at the age of sixty-five is preferable to dying bed-ridden at the age of ninety. To argue in this way is not to advocate a foolhardy approach to exercise as one ages, but rather to stress the facts that exercise can be extremely enjoyable and beneficial at any age; that there are built-in safety valves in the human being; that the nature or intensity of exercise will obviously change as one continues to play squash; and finally that there are warning signals which must be heeded, namely undue breathlessness or tiredness, anything abnormal with regard to the heart, and chest or arm pains. Immediately these danger signs manifest themselves, exercise must cease and a doctor should be consulted.

To somebody over the age of thirty who wishes to take up squash, it is probably a sensible precaution to have a thorough medical examination, especially if that person has not led a particularly active existence. Given the doctor's approval, the squash activity should be built up very gradually.

Anybody who has experienced serious health problems, in particular heart trouble, should only return to exercise under a doctor's supervision, and with caution.

Finally, no matter what your age, do not play when you are ill.

FUTURE OF SQUASH

Recently there have been calls for a re-think, amongst other things, as to the dimensions of the court. These calls seem to have arisen because promoters battle to sell the game to sponsors, the media and to the general public. Two of the more popular suggestions have been to lower the height of the tin which would make winners easier to hit, and to employ court markings similar to those in the American game which would make the lob more effective.

I am not in favour of changing the dimensions of the court, the adjustment to the outside lines being marginally less distasteful. The game of squash is a marvellous game thoroughly enjoyed by a great many players. To change the nature of the game to fill the odd squash court gallery on infrequent occasions is not sensible. There is some merit in changing the height of the tin or the scoring system for a specific tournament with a view to gaining more publicity and maybe to attract an increased number of spectators. I believe squash to be largely a participants' sport with spectator appeal being limited by the size of the ball and the speed at which it is struck, and by the very nature of the game. The former reason explains why the game does not televise particularly well and the nature of the game may limit interest in squash to the initiated.

Probably the most significant break-through recently in court construction has been the use of portable courts, especially the all-glass type. The match court may now be erected in, for example, a theatre or auditorium. This has appreciably improved the number of spectators at a major event. With more people watching, sponsorships should improve. This flow of money into the game is likely to benefit mainly the top strata of players, who are by no means undeserving, but perhaps more effort should be devoted to ways in which squash can be played by more people at a lower cost.

SPIRIT OF THE GAME

'O friends, be men, and let your
  hearts be strong.
And let no warrior in the heat of
  fight,
Do what may bring him shame in
  others' eyes.' (Homer)

Geoff Hunt was a great world champion. His athleticism, his quiet, self-effacing character and his sincere interest in the game of squash ensures many admirers for him throughout the world. Geoff was scrupulously honest on court and played the game not only according to the rules but also according to the spirit of the game. The men responsible for the rules of the game have tried to formalize this spirit but, given the average experience and capability of referees, have failed. In any event, their task was almost impossible without dealing with individual circumstances which would make the rules and explanations far too lengthy.

Intimidation plays a part in most sports. The use of the bouncer in cricket immediately springs to mind. In squash, the intimidation of the opponent should only be achieved by the daunting prospect of his having to run faster and farther than his condition allows. The players, even (or rather especially) when competing for money, must continuously and consciously recognize that the arena is a confined space, that the opponent must not be intimidated by excessive and dangerous swings of the racket, and that he must be given an early and direct path to the ball with sufficient space in which to play his shot.

111

MAGIC

The magic of this game is enhanced by remembering that excuses are irrelevant and that a winner should always be allowed to enjoy his victory. If this book increases your enjoyment, it has been a resounding success. I leave you with a comment attributed to a former South African champion: 'Squash is a simple game—you just have to hit the ball tighter and tighter and tighter!'